TOMBSTONE

J. M. Thompson
and
Fred Bean

A SIGNET BOOK

SIGNET
Published by New American Library, a division of
Penguin Putnam Inc., 375 Hudson Street,
New York, New York 10014, U.S.A.
Penguin Books Ltd, 27 Wrights Lane,
London W8 5TZ, England
Penguin Books Australia Ltd, Ringwood,
Victoria, Australia
Penguin Books Canada Ltd, 10 Alcorn Avenue,
Toronto, Ontario, Canada M4V 3B2
Penguin Books (N.Z.) Ltd, 182–190 Wairau Road,
Auckland 10, New Zealand

Penguin Books Ltd, Registered Offices:
Harmondsworth, Middlesex, England

First published by Signet, an imprint of New American Library,
a division of Penguin Putnam Inc.

First Printing, May 2001
10 9 8 7 6 5 4 3 2 1

PUBLISHER'S NOTE
Some of the selections in this book are works of fiction. Names, characters, places,
and incidents either are the product of the author's imagination or are used fictitiously,
and any resemblance to actual persons, living or dead, events, or locales is entirely
coincidental.

During the writing of this novel, I lost three of my best friends: my father, Jim Thompson, my big "brother," William Boudreaux, and my faithful and loving companion of fourteen years, my dog, Clancy. I will miss them all. *Adios, amigos. Vaya con Dios!*

JMT

Prologue:

Prelude to a Gunfight

Tombstone, Arizona, was a rowdy, freewheeling frontier town in December 1879 when the Earp brothers arrived. Less than a year old, the town was a dusty, windblown collection of tents and wooden clapboard shacks nestled on a high plateau between the Dragoon and Whetstone mountains of the Arizona desert.

The main attraction of the town to the Earps was the immense amount of silver coming out of the nearby San Pedro Hills. The miners needed someplace close by to spend their newfound wealth and to get supplies. The streets swarmed with miners and prospectors, merchants opening shops, prostitutes plying their trade, confidence men and footpads loitering around waiting to pounce on tenderfeet and pilgrims to sell them worthless mines or land well away from the rich silver fields in the hills just out of town. To the Earps, this was a town begging for someone to come in and make a fortune from the many opportunities it presented.

The three Earp brothers—Wyatt, Virgil, and James—arrived in town wearing long black frock coats, stiff-brimmed black hats, and boiled white shirts with string ties. They looked more like traveling preachers than lawmen.

James, tired of being a lowly bartender, soon became immersed in his new occupation as a saloonkeeper. He wanted no part of the rough-and-ready game of being a lawman.

Virgil, who'd been sworn in as a deputy U.S. marshal while on the way to Tombstone, was almost immediately drawn to the law when the city marshal was shot and killed by a cattle rustler. Virgil was assigned to the post and accepted the full-time job, giving up his dream of prospecting on the side.

Wyatt bought into a gambling concession at the best saloon in town, the Oriental, in addition to dealing faro at another establishment across the street at night, the Eagle Brewery.

He somehow also had time to work as a deputy sheriff and somewhat later as Virgil's assistant city marshal.

Some months later, the three Earps were joined in Tombstone by a fourth brother, Morgan. With Wyatt's help, Morgan hired on as shotgun rider for Wells, Fargo on the Tucson stage run.

The Earps were pleased when an old friend of

Wyatt's from his Dodge City days, John Holliday, arrived in town. A hard-drinking dentist who suffered from tuberculosis, Holliday was quick tempered and always looking to pick a fight.

As might be expected, the Earps soon ran afoul of forces in Tombstone that wanted the town to be wide open with little interference from the law, primarily the ranchers and cowboys and rustlers who lived outside of the city limits.

The most vocal proponents of letting the town remain uncontrolled were two sets of brothers, the Clantons and McLaurys. The two clans were involved in both cattle raising and cattle rustling, selling their beef to the Army as well as customers in Tombstone.

There were clashes between the Earps and the brothers because of their propensity to rustle cattle, mules, and even on one occasion Wyatt's own prized race horse.

The Clantons and McLaurys managed to get away with their thievery in large part because of their friendship and possible partnership with John Behan, the sheriff of Cochise County, of which Tombstone was the county seat. Behan needed the votes of the cowboys and ranchers of the county in order to stay in office, as well as enjoying his share of the profits from their cattle-stealing businesses.

This setup, with Behan and the cowboys controlling the county and the Earps the town, led to inevitable conflict.

In September 1881, Virgil arrested one of Behan's deputies, Frank Stilwell, along with a friend of the Clantons, Pete Spence, for holding up a stage. Behan posted bail for the defendants. Frank McLaury, another friend of Spence's, came into town when he heard of the arrest.

Upon seeing Morgan Earp on the street, Frank McLaury, backed up by Ike Clanton, told him, "If you ever come after *me*, you'll never take me!"

The Earps took this as a challenge to their authority and began to plan for the inevitable showdown.

On October 25, Ike Clanton and Tom McLaury arrived in Tombstone. Billy Clanton and Frank McLaury were due in town the next day. Ike began making the rounds of various saloons in town, drinking heavily until well past midnight. Around one in the morning, he entered the Alhambra Saloon and ordered something to eat.

In the rear of the room, Wyatt and Morgan Earp watched his arrival with interest. Shortly thereafter, Doc Holliday walked in, taking a break from his nightly gambling and drinking.

Becoming enraged at the sight of his sworn enemy, Doc walked up to Ike's table and yelled, "You son-of-a-bitch cowboy, get out your gun and get to work!"

"I don't have any gun," Ike said, standing up, as angry as Doc.

Morgan, who was acting policeman at the time, decided to separate the pair and took Doc by the arm and pulled him outside to cool down.

When Ike came out after finishing his meal, Doc was waiting for him on the boardwalk. "You ain't heeled. Go heel yourself," he snarled. Morgan, who liked Ike even less than Doc, added, "You can have all the fight you want now."

Ike protested he was unarmed and walked off to find another poker game to occupy his time.

On October 26, the next morning, Ned Boyle, the bartender of the Oriental Saloon, was stopped on the street by Ike Clanton, now armed with a rifle and a six-shooter. He told Boyle, "As soon as those damned Earps make their appearance on the street today, the ball will open!"

Boyle went to Wyatt's room, woke him up, and told him of Ike's threat. Wyatt got dressed and went to find Virgil.

Soon, he and Virgil went looking for Ike. The outcome was now fixed.

Virgil saw Ike in an alley, sneaked up behind him, and grabbed his rifle. As the outraged Ike spun around, Virgil coldcocked him across the forehead with his pistol, knocking Ike to the ground.

Virgil stood over him. "You been hunting for me?" he asked.

"If I'd seen you a second sooner, I'd've killed you," Ike snarled back, holding a hand to his bleeding head.

Virgil arrested Ike for carrying a firearm in the city limits, and he and Morgan took Ike to the courthouse to press charges.

As the charges were being prepared, Wyatt ran into Tom McLaury outside the courtroom. McLaury said, "If you want to make a fight, I'll make a fight with you anywhere."

Wyatt drew his gun. "All right, make a fight right here," he said, slapping McLaury across the face with his left hand and with his right hitting him in the head with the barrel of his pistol.

McLaury fell unconscious to the ground and Wyatt walked calmly off down the street.

Billy Claibourne, a friend of the Clantons and McLaurys, appeared at the courthouse, helped Ike pay his fine, and took him to a doctor's office to get his head bandaged. After he left Ike, Billy ran into Billy Clanton and Frank McLaury and told them what had happened.

Billy Clanton, used to bailing his more hot-headed brother out of trouble, said, "I want Ike to go home. I didn't come here to fight anyone, and no one wants to fight me."

When Ike showed up, fresh bandages on his head, Billy Clanton said, "Get on your horse and go home."

As a crowd began to gather, Sheriff Behan, having heard of the trouble, hurried over to Virgil Earp. He assured the Earps he was going to disarm the cowboys and asked them not to start anything until he had a chance to do so.

Shortly after he left, bystanders told the Earps the cowboys were still on Fremont Street and still armed. The Earps announced they were going to arrest the Clantons and McLaurys and walked toward Fremont.

As Virgil, Morgan, and Wyatt walked down the center of the street, Doc Holliday followed a short distance behind.

"Doc, this ain't your fight," Wyatt called over his shoulder.

"That's a hell of a thing for you to say to me," Doc said. Virgil stopped, deputized Doc, and took his cane and handed him his own shotgun. Doc placed the shotgun under his coat out of sight and the four men continued their search for the Clantons and McLaurys.

The Clantons and McLaurys were gathered on the sidewalk at the corner of Fourth Street where it joined Fremont, near Camillus Fry's place, a lodging house and photography studio. Sheriff Behan was trying to persuade them to give up their guns. Ike Clanton said he wasn't armed, as did Tom McLaury.

Both Billy Clanton and Frank McLaury were wearing pistols, and a rifle hung in a rifle boot on Frank's horse.

When Behan told them to give him their arms, Frank said he should go to hell. Behan shook his head in frustration and told them to stay there, and he rushed up the street toward the approaching Earps.

When he got to them, he implored Virgil, "Earp, for God's sake, don't go down there."

"I'm going to disarm them!" Virgil growled.

The Earps and Doc Holliday pushed past Behan. "Go back. I'm sheriff of this county!" he shouted and followed them.

As the Earps and Holliday reached Fry's place, the Clantons and McLaurys backed up until their backs were against the wall of a house, Frank holding the reins of his horse next to him.

The Earps stepped forward until they were no more than six feet from the others, Virgil in front.

Billy Clanton and Frank McLaury let their hands fall to their holstered pistols.

"Hold! I want your guns," Virgil Earp called out.

Someone shouted, "Son of a bitch!"

Shots rang out as the battle began.

Billy Clanton aimed his pistol at Wyatt. Wyatt, with a lightning-fast move, drew a six-shooter from under his coat and fired at Frank McLaury just as Billy let go at Wyatt.

Billy's shot went wild. Wyatt's slug took McLaury in the stomach, doubling him over as he staggered up the street, groaning in pain and shock.

When he saw his brother hit, Tom McLaury threw open his vest, shouting, "I have nothing!"

He then whirled, grabbing for Frank's rifle as he took cover behind his brother's horse.

Morgan whipped his pistol out and fired at Billy Clanton twice. One bullet shattered Billy's right wrist; the other struck him in the chest. Blown backward, he stumbled and fell back against the wall of the house. As he slid down the wall to the ground, he switched his pistol from his right hand to his left. Lying there, against the wall, he continued to fire wildly at the Earps.

Billy's brother, Ike Clanton, rushed at Wyatt and grabbed his arm. Wyatt, seeing he was unarmed, pushed him away. "Go to fighting or get away," Wyatt growled.

Ike let go of Wyatt's arm and ran toward Fry's front door, a shotgun blast by Doc narrowly missing him as he dove through the doorway.

Frightened by the gunfire, Frank McLaury's horse bolted, exposing Tom McLaury. Doc Holliday aimed his double-barreled shotgun and let go with the second barrel. The buckshot tore a fist-size hole in Tom's chest and side, and he staggered a few steps before he fell to the ground, dying.

Virgil, who hadn't fired a shot yet, was knocked to the ground, a bullet from Billy Clanton tearing into his calf. Clanton, meanwhile, was still lying on the ground firing.

Frank McLaury, blood pouring from his stomach, grabbed at his horse as it ran by, trying to get his rifle out of the saddle scabbard. He missed the rifle, but drew his pistol and whirled to find Doc Holliday staring at him over the barrel of his own pistol.

The two men fired at the same time.

Frank McLaury fell, a bullet hole just under his ear.

Doc stumbled, his hip pierced by McLaury's bullet.

Billy, lying on the ground bleeding, fired his last shot at Morgan, hitting him in the shoulder. As Morgan was blown sideways and fell, Billy tried to get to his feet.

Morgan rolled to the side and fired from the ground, at the same time as Wyatt. Hit under the ribs, Billy Clanton collapsed again. He lay on the ground dying, still trying to cock his empty six gun. "Give me some more cartridges," he pleaded.

Then the shooting stopped. Of the eight men involved, three were dead and three were wounded. Only Ike Clanton, who had run out the back of Fry's to take refuge in a Mexican dance hall on Allen Street, and Wyatt Earp remained untouched.

From first shot to last, the entire battle had

lasted less than a minute, but its repercussions were to be felt throughout Tombstone for months to come.

The battle between the cowboys and the Earps was over, but the war was just beginning. . . .

Chapter 1

Dr. Alexandre Leo LeMat was reading a week-old
copy of the *Tombstone Daily Epitaph* containing a
report by John Gosper, Acting Governor of the
Territory of Arizona in the absence of John C. Fremont, to the U.S. Secretary of State regarding the
bloodbath in October of 1881 in Cochise County,
Arizona Territory. The shootout that had occurred
had quickly taken on the name "the Battle at the
O.K. Corral." Leo's companion of many years,
Jacques LeDieux, listened while Leo read aloud.

"The headline reads 'Yesterday's Tragedy,' then
it says, 'Three Men Hurled Into Eternity in the
Duration of a Moment.'"

Jacques continued preparing their breakfast
over a wood stove in Leo's suite on the top floor
of the Saint Anthony Hotel in San Antonio, fold-
ing cheese and Cajun spices into an omelette that
would be added to the paper-thin crêpes he already had on a plate beside a bowl of strawberry
jam. "I will never understand your fascination

with killing or these Western gunmen, Leo,"
Jacques said. "You will ruin my appetite with
these stories. There must be something else worth
reading in that dreadful newspaper. Did we not
see enough of killings and shootings when we
were boys growing up in New Orleans?"

"Listen to the report given by the acting governor," Leo continued, ignoring his friend's request.
"This was written a month before the shooting at
the O.K. Corral. He was outraged by the criminal
activity which he found in Cochise County."

Leo shook the newspaper flat and proceeded to
read the account.

> The cowboy element at times very fully pre-
> dominates, and the officers of the law are either
> unable or unwilling to control this class of out-
> laws, sometimes being governed by fear, at other
> times by a hope of reward. At Tombstone, the
> county seat of Cochise County, I conferred with
> the sheriff upon the subject of breaking up these
> bands of outlaws, and I am sorry to say he gave
> me but little hope of being able in his department
> to cope with the power of these cowboys.
>
> He represented to me that the deputy U.S.
> marshal, resident of Tombstone, and the city
> marshal for the same, seemed unwilling to
> heartily cooperate with him in capturing and
> bringing to justice these outlaws.
>
> In conversation with the deputy U.S. marshal,
> Mr. Earp, I found precisely the same spirit of
> complaint existing against Mr. Behan, the sheriff,

and his deputies. Many of the very best law-abiding and peace-loving citizens have no confidence in the willingness of the civil officers to pursue and bring to justice that element of outlawry so largely disturbing the sense of security, and so often committing highway robbery and smaller thefts. The opinion is quite prevalent in Tombstone and elsewhere in the vicinity of that part of the Territory that the civil officers are largely in league with the leaders of this disturbing and dangerous element.

Something must be done, and that right early, or very grave results will follow. It is an open disgrace to American liberty and the peace and the security of her citizens, that such a state of affairs could exist.

Jacques placed the omelettes on plates. "So what do you find so unique about dishonest lawmen who turn their backs on crime?" he asked. "We saw it most of our young lives on the wharfs, didn't we? Crooked policemen with their hands out for bribes were a daily occurrence there."

"This marshal . . . Wyatt Earp. He seems to be cut from a different cloth. Listen to what else the *Daily Epitaph* has to say about him."

Jacques made a face, one that twisted the deep scar down his cheek, the result of an old knife wound. "I have this feeling that Marshal Wyatt Earp has captured your imagination, Leo. Please tell me we are not bound for Tombstone and the deserts of Arizona Territory so you can paint his portrait."

"And what would it matter, *mon ami,* if this was our destination?"

"Arizona Territory is even more primitive than Kansas, where you became so fascinated with Wild Bill Hickok. Kansas is the most terrible place I've ever been, only I hear that Arizona is worse . . . if such a thing is possible."

Leo chuckled. Their trip to Abilene in Kansas Territory had been eventful, to say the least, and meeting Marshal Wild Bill Hickok had been a study in contrasts. Hickok was a boastful fellow, but not without deadly talents that had earned him his reputation in frontier cattle towns.

"Listen to this," Leo continued. "'Apparently this United States Deputy Marshal Wyatt Earp is quite bold, as is the man they call Doc Holliday, a dentist by trade, who this reporter says is possessed with an ungovernable temper and was given both to drinking and quarreling.'"

Jacques let out a soft sigh of resignation, for he felt sure he knew where this was leading them.

Leo continued reading.

At eleven in the morning, Marshal Earp was awakened by Ned Boyle, a bartender at the Oriental Saloon where Marshal Earp made additional income by dealing faro.

A fellow by the name of Ike Clanton, who had two brothers named Phineas and Billy, joined forces with two brothers named Frank and Tom McLaury. But there were three Earp brothers—Wyatt, Virgil, and Morgan—to be dealt with as officers of the law.

"It sounds like a Cajun family gathering," Jacques said, bringing Leo's plate over to the dining room table, "the kind that usually ends up with knives being drawn."

"It grows even more fascinating. Doc Holliday, a gunfighter of some reputation, was with the Earp brothers. The Clantons and the McLaurys, along with a friend and fellow cowboy by the name of Billy Claiborne, got into an argument and they met on Freemont Street with guns blazing."

"This must have been close to the O.K. Corral," Jacques observed, sitting down in front of his own plate.

"Yes," Leo said, frowning down the page, "very close to it. In fact, only half a block away. There's a crude sketching of a map of the area on the next page."

"What started the shooting?" Jacques asked.

"A simple command made by Sheriff John Behan. He first asked the Clantons and McLaurys to disarm themselves. When they refused, saying they would not give up their guns until the Earps and Doc Holliday did likewise, Sheriff Behan asked the Earp brothers and Doc Holliday to surrender their weapons to him at once."

"Why would a sheriff try to disarm peace offi-
cers who were legally allowed to carry firearms?"
Jacques inquired, tasting his spicy omelette.
"Mais ça c'est fou! . . . It is crazy," he added in the
Cajun tongue they both learned as children in
New Orleans.

"It doesn't say, Jacques. But things began to
happen very rapidly after that. Billy Clanton fired
the first shot at Wyatt Earp. Wyatt apparently ignored the attack by Billy Clanton and drew his
six-shooter, firing at Frank McLaury. Billy Clanton missed. Wyatt Earp didn't, hitting Frank
McLaury somewhere in the chest or stomach region, mortally wounding him."

"Mon Dieu," Jacques whispered.

"Tom McLaury," Leo continued, "seeing his
brother struck by a bullet, pulled his pistol. But as
this was happening, Billy Clanton, the first man
to fire a shot, was hit by a bullet from Morgan
Earp's pistol. He fell back against a window of
the Harwood house.

"Ike Clanton, deciding to save his own skin,
took off at a run toward the door of an establishment called Fry's Photography Gallery.

"Then Doc Holliday took aim at Tom McLaury.
He hit him in the chest. Tom staggered down Fremont Street a few steps and then fell down, dying.

"Virgil Earp felt a bullet tear into the calf of his
leg, a shot fired by the wounded Billy Clanton.
Virgil fell to the ground. However, the badly

wounded Frank McLaury was not yet out of the fight. He drew a hidden gun, only to find Doc Holliday standing over him.

"Doc fired at McLaury at the same time a shot was fired at McLaury by Morgan Earp. McLaury crumpled with a bullet hole below his ear, but the shot McLaury got off pierced Doc Holliday's hip."

Jacques wagged his head. "That does remind me of the parties we used to have on the banks of Bayou Rouge. Everyone is shooting someone," he said. "By the way, your omelette is getting cold, *mon ami*."

"I'm almost finished reading this," Leo said. "Listen to the last paragraph of this reporter's account. He says here that Billy Clanton, mortally wounded and lying against a building, fired the last shot. His target was Morgan Earp, and he managed to hit him in the right shoulder. Morgan stumbled and fell. Billy Clanton then tried to get to his feet and he was shot dead by Wyatt Earp."

Jacques seemed to know what was coming next. "Shall I contact the Southern and Pacific Railroad to make arrangements for your private car to be coupled to the next passenger train to Tombstone?"

Leo rested the *Tombstone Daily Epitaph* on his lap, gazing out a hotel window. "Not quite yet," he said a moment later. "First I've got to wire

Marshal Wyatt Earp to see if he will agree to sit for a portrait."

Jacques chewed thoughtfully on his crêpe. "As a physician, you have the training to save men's lives, under most circumstances. Yet you carry your uncle's patented LeMat revolver and seem to look for any excuse to use it. On top of that, you have what many regard—including the famous portraitist, George Catlin, who trained you in the arts—a gift for painting portraits. But this preoccupation you have with Western gunfighters is beyond me. Why do you only wish to paint them?"

Leo got up and came over to the table, inhaling deeply of the aroma given off by Jacques's delicious omelettes. He surveyed the white linen tablecloth and fine china plates and cups before he sat down. "I agree it's a strange fascination, Jacques," he said, spreading his napkin over his lap. "However, there's something about these Western killers. . . ."

"And what might that be? Most of them are common ruffians, in my experience."

Leo bit into his strawberry jam–laden crêpe before he took the time to reply. "They have a certain quality I admire . . . the courage to face men with a gun, often in one-sided duels where the odds are stacked heavily against them."

"Perhaps they are only fools," Jacques suggested. "I found Wild Bill Hickok to be something of a fraud. His reputation far exceeds his skill with a pistol."

"I tend to agree, although Hickok accomplished most of his acts of courage when he was drunk, as we both learned while we were in Kansas."

Jacques nodded. "Quite possibly this Wyatt Earp is cut from the same alcohol-soaked cloth."

"Perhaps. We won't know until we get there."

"This means we *are* going to Tombstone, I take it?"

"Only if the marshal agrees to sit for me. I'll prepare a telegram to be sent off today."

"I hear it is even hotter in Arizona Territory than it was in Kansas this summer," Jacques lamented.

Leo gave Jacques a look of mock irritation. "You seem to be continually complaining about the weather, Monsieur LeDieux. If we were in Egypt, where those marvelous pyramids are now being explored, I might understand. Egypt is hot, but to be given the opportunity to see what is inside those burial chambers would be a price I'd willingly pay. I just read in *Harpers Magazine* about an archaeological expedition from London beginning a dig at the pyramids, despite the terrible heat."

"Tombstone sounds worse," Jacques said, spearing the last bite of his crêpe. "I suppose I should begin packing our trunks. . . ."

* * *

After he put away the dishes, Jacques began packing for the trip to Tombstone. As usual, in addition to the clothes and sundries he and Leo would need, he filled one entire trunk with Leo's art supplies and canvasses, and another trunk with various weapons and ammunition. Leo had several varieties of the famous LeMat pistols his uncle had invented.

The pistols consisted of nine-shot revolvers with a central shotgun barrel, approximately twenty gauge in size. The pistols had been prized by the Confederate officers who had used them exclusively in the War Between the States; they were known far and wide as the most deadly handguns ever made.

Jacques also packed his beloved Ange, a twelve-gauge double-barreled shotgun he preferred over more conventional weapons.

After the trunks were packed, he called a boy from the hotel to take them to the train station across town. Leo kept his private coach parked on a side line there for occasions such as this when he desired to travel across the country.

Wealthy from his share of his uncle's royalties on the LeMat weapons, Leo also made quite a good living painting portraits of individuals who wished to be immortalized by his prodigious talents as an artist. Though he hated this sort of painting, the fees, which ranged upward of several thousand dollars, gave Leo the financial freedom to indulge his other passion—painting notorious outlaws and lawmen of the West—and to occasionally hire out his gun for the protection of those he thought needed it.

Jacques had the boy put the trunks in the rear of the private coach in the luggage compartment, then began to see that the attached kitchen was properly stocked for the trip.

Jacques did not intend for Leo and him to be at the mercy of anyone else's cooking on the long journey to Arizona. He stocked the cupboards with fresh vegetables, eggs, butter, and other necessities of his craft. The meat he would buy along the way, having no way to keep it fresh on the train.

Once he was satisfied all necessary preparations had been made, he poured himself a brandy and sat in one of the easy chairs in the coach, putting his feet up on a coffee table and leaning his head back.

As he sipped the brandy, he let his mind wander back to other adventures he and Leo had shared, wondering just what they were going to encounter in the wilds of Arizona.

He knew one thing: if it was like their other trips, it would be anything but boring.

Chapter 2

The three bodies lay at Ritter and Ream Undertaking Parlor across the street from the Oriental Saloon in Tombstone. Tom and Frank McLaury, as well as Billy Clanton, rested in silver-trimmed caskets. Visitors came by to glimpse the corpses from time to time. The three funerals were planned for the following day.

Wyatt Earp sat at a window table of the Oriental while he listened to Magistrate Court Judge Wells Spicer recount the events Wyatt knew all too well. It was a blistering hot afternoon in southern Arizona Territory. Winds gusted up and down the business district, sending clouds of dust into the hot, dry air of late fall.

"Of the eight men involved in this bloody feud, ain't but two of you who isn't dead or wounded," Judge Spicer said, holding a Bible against his chest, standing across from Wyatt's table in slanted rays of afternoon sun. It was a fact, al-

though it was nothing Wyatt needed to be reminded of.

"I can count," Wyatt said, his eyes on the street
of a quiet town perched on a high plateau between the Dragoon and Whetstone mountain
ranges. "There's still a bunch of 'em out there
who need killing . . . Curly Bill Brocius, Ike Clanton, Johnny Ringo, and the rest of the yellow bastards who call themselves 'the cowboys.' My
brothers, Morgan an' Virgil, have got cowards'
bullets in 'em. Why aren't you doing something
about that? Morgan has a bullet in his shoulder.
Virgil has a slug in his leg. Doc has a bullet hole
through his hip."

"You went looking for trouble," the judge said,
as if it were cold, hard fact.

Wyatt's eyes narrowed as he looked at Judge
Spicer. "That's horseshit and you know it. The
Clantons and McLaurys wanted this fight. We
gave it to 'em."

"But you were officers of the law, Wyatt. Virgil
is a deputy U.S. marshal.

Wyatt nodded. "And that gave him the authority to disarm those boys. Morgan is chief of police
in Tombstone. Behan is the sheriff of Cochise
County, and yet he was sidin' with the Clantons
and McLaurys. What kind of lawman does that
make him, Judge?"

"He was only recently appointed by the acting
governor, Wyatt, as you know. He faces an elec-

tion soon. I wrote the governor recently that Tombstone gave all signs of acquiring a civilized gloss. Not long ago, Tombstone had only two dance halls, at least a dozen gambling places and more than twenty saloons. Still, I told the governor there was hope. Now we have Julius Caesar's New York Coffee House and the Cosmopolitan Hotel's Maison Doree, where a brisket of good beef *a la flambé* can be purchased, along with ham in champagne sauce. The Bird Cage is staging a production of *Pinafore*, and after the performance you have a choice of two ice cream parlors to patronize. This is the mark of advancing civilization."

"You're tellin' me things I already know, Judge," Wyatt said.

"Then why would you turn our quest for a civilized city into a nightmare by engaging in this bloody gunfight? These killings at the O.K. Corral have made news all across the country, so I have been told."

Wyatt sighed heavily. "You know damn well these cowboys are crooks and livestock thieves. They went too far this time, and as peace officers, someone had to stop them. That's what me an' my brothers are bein' paid to do—to enforce the laws of this town and the territory."

"You have a strange way of doing it. A rather violent method, I might add."

"What the hell did you want us to do? Quite

clearly, the control of this town, the town you believe is so civilized, is gained by disarming rowdy cowboys who violate the laws and carry guns. The editor of the *Tombstone Nugget* wrote recently that things had gotten out of hand."

"Out of hand?"

"Apparently you didn't read his column, Judge. He wrote that after dark, things were getting so violent that on a Sunday night, a bunch of 'lewd women' and their men friends—meaning these so-called cowboys—held an impromptu street celebration with blazing six-shooters on Fremont Street. He said that we mostly live in canvas houses here, and with lunatics like those cowboys who fired so promiscuously the other night, it ain't safe anyhow."

"I did not read that particular editorial. However, we have no proof, other than the word of the editor of the *Nugget*, that this particular incident can be traced to the cowboys in actual fact."

"You believe whatever you want, Judge," Wyatt said, weary of this discussion. "Only any fool with one eye can see it wasn't a bunch of school kids doin' the shooting."

Spicer cleared his throat. "Proof of a solid nature is required in a court of law as to who might be responsible for these actions."

"I intend to get you that proof, Judge."

"And how do you intend to do that, Marshal Earp?" he asked.

"We have witnesses . . . men who are willing to testify as to who fired the first shot. Billy Clanton and his trigger-happy gun started the whole thing."

"You may need those witnesses," the judge declared after a glance out the front window.

"Why is that, Judge?"

Spicer seemed unwilling to answer at first. "Because I am told that Sheriff Behan and a number of citizens intend to file charges against you."

"File charges?" Wyatt was surprised. "Hell, half the population of this town saw what happened . . . that Billy Clanton fired the first shot. It was Virgil's and my intention only to disarm them."

"There are others who are willing to testify otherwise, Wyatt."

Wyatt scowled. "You mean other cowboys like Curly Bill and Johnny Ringo."

"There are others."

"There's no jury in the world who would take the word of Curly Bill or Ringo over that of me and my brothers. And you know Sheriff Behan is in cahoots with them, turning his back when they break the law."

"There may be no choice but to settle this in court, Wyatt. It won't be my idea."

Marshal Earp came suddenly to his feet, an icy look in his eyes. "Then let the bastards bring their charges against us, Judge."

Spicer raised his Bible as if in defense and backed away from Wyatt's table. "There is no need to become so enraged by what I said."

"Like hell! If John Behan and Ike Clanton, along with Curly Bill and Ringo, can influence this whole town against us, then let them have their day in court . . . if me and my brothers don't kill 'em first."

"You shouldn't make threats like that, Wyatt," Spicer said, glancing over his shoulder to see if anyone was nearby. "Someone might overhear you."

"I don't give a damn if every citizen in Tombstone knows how I feel, Judge! My brothers damn near got killed trying to disarm a bunch of outlaws who flaunted the law, and now you tell me that *we* may have to stand trial for bringing them down?"

"It's possible," Spicer answered. "Behan is the sheriff of Cochise County and he can file charges against almost anyone who resides here."

"Behan is a goddamned crook and you know it. He's let these cowboys get away with all sorts of criminal activity."

"Can you prove that?" the judge asked timidly.

Wyatt's eyes narrowed even more. "I sure as hell intend to. Or I'll arrest the son of a bitch myself."

Spicer moved closer to the swinging doors of the Oriental Saloon. "That might not be a good idea, Marshal Earp. Not unless you can come up with concrete charges you can prove against him in court."

Wyatt stuck an unlit cheroot between his teeth. "I'll damn sure see what I can do about that, Judge. In the meantime, if you see Behan, you tell him he'd better be heeled if he runs into me."

"Heeled?"

"Armed. Carrying a goddamn gun."

"Do you mean to imply that you intend to kill the sheriff of this county?"

"He'd better not give me a reason to."

"That's strong talk, Marshal Earp."

Wyatt gave him a mirthless grin. "And I can sure back it up, Judge. You tell that skinny bastard when you see him that he'd better be carrying iron if he crosses trails with me, 'cause I *will* kill the son of a bitch if he brings any charges against me or my brothers."

"But as a peace officer, you are sworn to uphold the law, Mr. Earp."

"I'll toss this lousy badge in the first ditch I can find, so it'll just be me and Behan. You tell him what I said. He's a dead man if he brings any kind of charge against me, or Virgil, or Morgan over what happened at the O.K. Corral. That goes for any charges against Doc Holliday, too."

"I'd best be going," the judge said, moving quickly toward the front doors.

"Don't forget to tell Behan what I said."

"I will, only I think you've taken leave of your senses, Marshal."

"Maybe I have," Wyatt said around his unlit cigar. "I still mean every goddamn word of it. I'll get notice to Curly Bill and Ike Clanton. Johnny Ringo, too, if I can find him. This is just the beginning of the killing if they push things too far in this town."

Judge Spicer hurried out onto the boardwalk. Wyatt stood near the window watching Spicer stride down the street with his Bible under his arm.

Ned Boyle, bartender at the Oriental, had been listening to the entire conversation. "I'd be real careful of them cowboys, Wyatt. Most especially that sneaky bastard Johnny Ringo. He's liable to back-shoot you from an alley late some night."

"Not if I kill the lowly cur first," Wyatt said as he turned for the bar. "Pour me a whiskey, Ned."

A barefoot boy in knickers and a tattered shirt brought Wyatt the telegram from San Antonio. Wyatt gave the kid a few copper coins before he opened the wire.

"I'll be damned," he said moments later.

"What is it?" Ned asked from his place behind the long mahogany bar.

"Some guy who calls himself Dr. Leo LeMat wants to come to Tombstone to paint my picture.

He says here that he's a portraitist, whatever the hell that is."

Ned gave the street a thoughtful glance and remained quiet for a time. "I wonder if he's any relation to the New Orleans LeMats who invented the pistol," he finally said.

"A pistol?"

Ned nodded. "A very special gun. It was carried by my brother and other Confederate officers during the war. It fires nine rounds, and it has a shotgun barrel in the center of the cylinder. It was, and is, a deadly weapon at close range."

"It don't say anything about pistols in this telegram, Ned. All the guy wants to do is paint my picture, like I was somebody real famous."

"Will you agree to it?" Ned wondered aloud.

Wyatt thought about it. "I reckon so. Don't see any good reason not to . . . only I still can't figure why he'd want to paint me."

"You're makin' quite a name for yourself, Wyatt," Ned pointed out. "After Dodge City, an' now this shootin' here in Tombstone, a lot of folks know who you are. I hear even ol' Erastus Beadle is plannin' to write one of his dime novels about you and your brothers."

"That isn't exactly the kind of reputation I've been lookin' for all my life, Ned."

"You've established yourself as a tough lawman, Wyatt, an' that's what this part of the coun-

try needs—men who ain't afraid of these swag-
gerin' outlaws."

"I'm not afraid of 'em," Wyatt said, "but a stray
bullet can end damn near any man's life if he happens to be standing in the wrong spot."

"I understand," Ned replied, putting more
clean glasses on a shelf behind the bar. "I wouldn't
trade places with you for all the money in Tombstone . . . or the whole damn territory, for that
matter."

Wyatt glanced at the telegram again, his mind
wandering away from what had happened on
Fremont Street a few days ago. "It still sounds
real damn silly for a man to want to come all the
way from Texas just to paint my picture."

"Hell, Wyatt, after what happened at the O.K.
Corral, you're on the way to bein' a famous man."

Wyatt shook his head. "I don't feel all that
damn famous, Ned. Right now, after what happened to Doc and my brothers, I feel lucky just to
be alive."

After the judge left, Wyatt finished his whiskey,
threw some money on the table, and made his
way to the rooms where the Earps and their
wives were holed up. They'd all moved in together until they could see which way the wind
was going to blow after the gunfight. The brothers wanted their wives safe, and they wanted to

be able to watch one another's backs in case the cowboys tried to come after them for vengeance.

He nodded at his wife, Josie, and Virgil's wife, Allie, as they sat in the parlor. Then he made his way to Morgan's bedroom, pausing at the door and watching as Morgan's wife sponged his sweaty brow with a cool cloth.

Lou looked over her shoulder when she heard him enter the room.

He crossed to the bed and sat gingerly on the edge, putting his hand on Morgan's right shoulder. Bloody bandages covered the left shoulder where the bullet had entered.

"How's he doin'?" he asked, not liking the way Morgan's skin was pale and flushed and covered with sweat.

Lou shook her head, tears brimming in her eyes. "I don't know, Wyatt. I'm afraid the wound's getting infected, and he doesn't seem to be able to move his left arm at all."

"Has the doc been by?"

"Yes, but he just says it's in God's hands now. He said if the bullet shattered the bone he may have to take the arm off," she finished, bursting into tears.

"That ain't gonna happen, Lou," Wyatt said, his jaw set. "Morg's gonna be just fine. He's strong as a bull. No little slug from that bastard Clanton is gonna put him in the dirt."

Chapter 3

Jacques and Leo stood next to their private coach as it sat near the end of a train bound for Fort Worth. Jacques had seen to the loading of their luggage while Leo kept a careful eye on a growing commotion half a block from the depot. A crowd had gathered around two men who were having an angry discussion on Presa Street. Both men had pistols tied down low on their hips.

Jacques came up behind Leo quietly, his boots making almost no sound on the red brick passenger platform.

"What is it?" Jacques asked.

"The beginnings of a fight, possibly a duel," Leo replied. "Both men are armed, and there's no sign of a peace officer now. Unless I'm badly mistaken, the man with the handlebar mustache is a killer by the name of Bill Longley. I believe I recognize him from an artist's sketch on a Wanted poster decorating the wall of U.S. Marshal

Thomas's office. I can't be sure it's Bill Longley unless I get a closer look at him."

"I have never heard of him, *mon ami*," Jacques said, "but you say he is a killer? A wanted man?"

"If I'm correct about his identity."

A man standing on the platform not far away overheard Leo's remark. He wore a business suit and a straw panama hat. He looked a bit out of place in San Antonio, though his face was darkly tanned and wrinkled, as if he'd spent considerable time in the sun.

"Did you say one of those men could be Bloody Bill Longley?" the man asked.

Leo was distracted by the remark. He gave the stranger a closer inspection. "I only said he resembles a drawing I have seen of Longley. I've never met Mr. Longley before, nor can I be sure of this man's identity."

The gentleman smiled and came over, offering his hand while the sounds of angry voices from the street grew louder. "I am Henry Stanley," he said. "I'm a writer . . . a reporter for *Harpers Magazine*, the *New York Herald*, and several other newspapers and magazines."

"Leo LeMat," he said, accepting Stanley's palm. "Your name does sound familiar." As a voracious reader of newspapers and magazines, the name struck a chord in Leo's memory.

Stanley smiled. "I've done several stories about

these Wild West characters. Perhaps you read my piece on Wild Bill Hickok a few months ago?"

"Indeed I have," Leo said. "In fact, it was your article that led me and my associate to Abilene, in Kansas Territory, to paint his portrait."

"You are a painter?" Stanley asked, sounding a bit surprised.

"A portraitist. Let me give you one of my cards."

Leo handed Stanley a business card with a simple legend across it. "Dr. Alexandre Leo LeMat. Portraitist. Gun for Hire."

Stanley read the card and blinked, then he stared up into Leo's face. "Gun for hire?" he asked. "It seems that painting portraits and offering your services as a shootist are many worlds apart, LeMat. Are you also a medical doctor?"

"I have a diploma in the healing arts from the University of Pennsylvania, however I don't usually practice medicine. I'm most interested in capturing the right subjects on canvas. I haven't been a practicing surgeon for many years."

Stanley's fascination showed on his slender face. "Another unusual contradiction, Dr. LeMat. A painter of portraits who is a medical practitioner and a hired gun, according to your card. I find it quite odd, if you'll excuse the observation, that a man trained to heal the sick and injured would be willing to kill a man for money."

"It isn't quite that simple. . . ." Leo began, until

he heard a yell from Presa Street. People witnessing the argument were now backing away from
the two men as they squared off in what looked
like the onset of a duel of fast draws.

"These men," Jacques said softly, "they are set
to kill each other now."

"So it seems," Leo observed. "From what I've
read about Bill Longley, if that indeed is who he is,
it seems that very few men are his equal as pistol-
men. I don't recognize the other man."

Leo walked away from the train to be closer to
the duel as the man with the handlebar mustache
who resembled the sketch of Longley crouched
slightly.

Then the gunman spoke. "Go fer your gun,
Jake. I'm ready, an' I'm done talkin' to you."

"I'll kill you, Bloody Bill," the man named Jake
snarled. "I know you've got a mean reputation,
but you ain't never faced the likes of me."

"Then jerk that smokewagon an' go to work,
cowboy," Bill said. "I'm waitin' on you . . . let's
get this settled before the law shows up."

A hush fell over the crowd of onlookers as Leo
made his way to a corner of the road, out of the
line of fire. He noticed that Henry Stanley was
just behind him. Jacques stood off to one side in
the afternoon shadow cast by a porch across the
front of a dry goods store, his hand near the pistol he carried underneath his tattered seaman's

shirt. No stranger to gunfights himself, his eyes glittered in anticipation of a good show.

"This may be interesting," Stanley whispered, stopping beside Leo. "I've also heard a great deal about Bloody Bill Longley and his exploits. He is said to be a remorseless killer with no trace of a conscience."

Leo wondered why the absence of a conscience in a gunfighter troubled Stanley. "I suppose we'll know soon enough," he said, watching Longley closely, fascinated as always by the actions of western gunmen.

Longley's gaze was fixed on his adversary in the street like a snake eyeing a field mouse. They stood less than fifty feet apart in front of the old Cactus Saloon, a run-down drinking parlor in one of the worst parts of town.

Longley's opponent appeared to be a young cowboy, not yet in his thirties. If Longley was as good as his reputation, he would make short work of this man.

A horseman appeared riding south along Presa Street, and Leo recognized him at once. Dub Rogers, Texas Ranger in charge of the Rangers' post in San Antonio, trotted his sorrel toward the scene of the difficulty.

"That's Captain Rogers," Jacques said softly.

"I know," Leo replied. "He's a friend . . . a good lawman. I may have to take a hand in this if Dub looks like he needs backup."

Jacques sighed. "It seems wherever there is a gunfight of some kind, you are all too willing to take a hand in it, as you put it."

"Rogers is a dedicated man. Types like Bloody Bill Longley shouldn't be allowed to shorten his career as a Texas Ranger. I intend to do what I can to stop it."

"I've seen Rogers at work," Jacques said. "He seems perfectly able to take care of himself."

Henry Stanley listened to their conversation with a worried look on his face, keeping one eye on Longley and the cowboy named Jake. "But why would you intervene, Dr. LeMat? You are not a peace officer."

"For the sake of friendship, Mr. Stanley. Dub Rogers has done me a few favors since I moved here from New Orleans. I'll repay my debt to him, if the opportunity arises."

"Be very careful of Longley," Stanley warned. "He is one of the subjects I intend to write about, after I return from Tombstone and an interview with Wyatt Earp."

Leo gave Stanley a sideways glance. "Then you're also on your way to Arizona to meet Mr. Earp. That's why my associate and I are traveling to Tombstone."

"You wish to interview him?" Stanley asked.

"No," Leo said, keeping an eye on Bill Longley and the man he called Jake. "I intend to paint his portrait. I received a wire from him only yesterday, agreeing to sit for me.

"Then we'll be traveling the same rails together," Stanley observed. "I have booked passage to Fort Worth, then west to the town of Tucson, where I understand the balance of my journey must be conducted by coach, since the rail line to Tombstone is undergoing repairs."

Ranger Dub Rogers halted his horse in front of a hitch rail and swung down. He looped his reins around the rail and started toward the two men squared off against each other in the middle of Presa Street.

"Now hold on, boys," Rogers shouted, parting the crowd around the two gunmen. "There ain't gonna be no shootin' in my district. You gents settle your differences someplace else, but not here." He gave Longley a hard stare. "We don't need your kind in San Antone, Bloody Bill. Take your gunfightin' elsewhere."

Longley turned slightly to face Rogers. "Ain't no son of a bitch gonna tell me what to do, badge or no badge. If you're aimin' to git killed, this'll be the right place and the right time."

Leo had heard enough. Captain Rogers had shown him too many kindnesses for Leo to ignore the danger he faced from a rabid gunman like Bill Longley.

He stepped off the boardwalk where he and Jacques and Stanley had been witnessing the exchange, moving slowly so as not to attract too much attention, opening his coat to enable him to reach the LeMat pistol he carried in a shoulder holster under his left arm.

"I'm an officer of the law," Rogers said, halting when he saw and heard the menace in Longley's threat. "I'm ordering you to get on your horse and clear out of San Antone . . . otherwise I'm gonna put you in jail."

Leo smiled, realizing there was no backing down in a Texas Ranger.

Longley gave the lawman a one-sided grin. "You an' who else, Ranger?"

Leo had positioned himself so he was almost directly behind Bill Longley's back as the gunman's attention was focused solely on the Texas Ranger.

"Me," Leo said softly, easy to hear now that the crowd had grown silent.

Longley jerked his head back to see who had spoken, swivelling his head back and forth to keep an eye still fixed on Ranger Dub Rogers.

Leo nodded, touching the brim of his black flat-brim hat as he gave Longley a cold look. "That's right, Mr. Longley," Leo said. "I'm the one you'll have to deal with if you make a move for your gun."

"Who the hell are you?" Longley demanded.

"What difference do names make?" Leo said, his lips curled in a half-smile.

Longley's eyelids slitted. "You ain't even wearin' a goddamn gun," he said.

"Perhaps you need spectacles, Mr. Longley. I am carrying a gun, and I assure you that if you reach for yours, I'll kill you before you can clear leather."

Longley found himself caught in a potential cross fire between three adversaries—the man called Jake, Texas Ranger Dub Rogers, and this new stranger, dressed in a black split-tail frock coat and stovepipe boots with a flat-brim hat shading his eyes from the afternoon sun.

"You're bluffin'," Longley said, casting a wary glance around him.

Before Leo could reply, Dub Rogers spoke. "Glad you happened along, Doc LeMat. This is a feller folks call Bloody Bill Longley, an' he's earned himself quite a reputation for killin' people."

Leo gave the Ranger a weak smile. "I never was one to worry about another man's reputation, Dub. Just let the man go for his gun and we'll see if his mean reputation is justly deserved."

Longley's fingers curled near the grips of his Colt .44 and he hesitated, looking from Jake to the Texas Ranger to Leo. Leo could see the indecision in his expression, although the temptation was still plainly written on his face.

"Don't try it, Mr. Longley," Ranger Rogers warned. "The man standin' behind you is Leo LeMat. He carries one of his uncle's LeMat pistols. If he decides to use that center barrel, the one loaded with buckshot, we'll be pickin' up your remains with feed scoops. Won't be nothin' left of you but hair on the wall."

Longley's face changed. "My pappy carried a LeMat durin' the war," he said, the challenge missing from his voice now. "I fired that middle barrel a few times myself. . . ."

Out of habit, more of a reflex, Leo dipped his hand inside his suit coat and whipped out his Baby LeMat, a smaller version of the Confederate cavalry pistol his uncle François invented.

Longley remained frozen in the middle of Presa Street, from both the speed with which Leo had drawn his revolver and out of fear for the deadly gun now squarely aimed at his chest. He stared at the LeMat pistol in Leo's hand, ignoring the Ranger behind him.

"I'll give you a demonstration, Mr. Longley, since you've been wise enough to leave your sidearm in its holster. But I warn you that I have nine forty-four caliber shells with your name on them, if you are so foolish as to go for your weapon against me."

Leo turned the barrel of his LeMat toward a wooden water trough in front of the Cactus. He cocked the center barrel hammer and fired from the hip.

A thundering shot echoed up and down Presa. Splinters of wood flew away from the water trough, shattering the entire structure so that water poured onto the street. Nothing remained of the trough, save for scraps of fragmented two-by-fours.

Longley jumped, moving his hand away from his pistol butt as he watched the water stain the dirt a dark brown.

Leo aimed his gun at Longley. "And now, Mr. Longley, if you'll be so kind as to raise your hands in the air, the Texas Ranger will disarm you and take you to jail for disturbing the peace. Be very careful to keep your hands high. Otherwise, you have my assurance that I'll kill you. . . ."

Longley hesitated, his eyes flicking back and forth between Leo and Dub Rogers and the man called Jake. Finally, trying to put the best face he could on it, he gave a lopsided grin and raised his hands.

Ranger Dub Rogers took a pair of iron manacles from his belt and pulled Longley's hands behind him, snapping the handcuffs together with a loud metallic click.

Rogers glanced over his shoulder at Leo, shaking his head. "Leo, I been sayin' for some time I got to get me one of them pistols."

Leo smiled back. "Say the word, Dub, and I'll send one to Ranger headquarters in Austin with your name on it."

Rogers nodded. "Much obliged, Leo, much obliged."

Chapter 4

The steam locomotive whistle sounded as the last passengers boarded the train. Leo continued speaking to Henry Stanley as the Texas and Pacific prepared to depart for Fort Worth, where it would continue west to El Paso and Tucson. Bystanders who had witnessed the disarming of Bill Longley gave Leo wary looks as the train made ready to leave San Antonio.

"Feel free to join us in my private coach," Leo said. "I recall reading your piece on Dr. David Livingstone and your most difficult journey to East Africa. I find I'm fascinated by world travels. I've been reading about the discoveries in Egypt and the expeditions to excavate tombs many believe are hidden below the pyramids. It will shorten the miles we travel to hear your account of your journeys along the Nile and Congo. You must be a man of great courage."

Stanley bowed politely, speaking with a hint of Irish accent when he replied. "I would be delighted, Dr. LeMat, so long as you are willing to share some of your own exploits. I still find it more than slightly curious that a medical doctor would choose to paint portraits and sell his services as a shootist over the more modest practice of healing. When you brought Bloody Bill Longley into the hands of justice a few moments ago, you clearly demonstrated your own bravery. As I understand it, he is not a man to be taken lightly."

Leo led the way to their coach. "I had the advantage, Mr. Stanley. He was facing three men with guns. I merely gave him a demonstration of what could happen if he refused my request to surrender to the proper authorities. It was a minor incident, one that is best forgotten."

"Climb aboard," Jacques said, offering Stanley his arm to help him into the coach. "Once this iron beast begins to move, the air passing through our window will be cooler. I'll prepare drinks all around, or coffee if you prefer. We have good brandy and cigars, if you're so inclined."

"Brandy," Stanley said thankfully as he climbed into a plush, carpeted Pullman fitted with fine furniture and oil paintings hanging from polished wood walls. "And a cigar would also be nice." His attention was immediately drawn to the portrait of a very young dark-haired girl. But for the moment, he said nothing about the painting.

Leo pointed to upholstered chairs around a

table near the center of the car. "Take a seat, Mr. Stanley. Jacques will pour our brandy. I'm most interested in your search for Dr. Livingstone and the hardships you must have faced in that part of the African continent. As I understand it from my readings, East Africa is wild, mostly unexplored country. And I'm told it is rife with little-known diseases."

Stanley took a chair while Jacques went to the back of the car for rum-soaked cheroots and brandy. "It was," he said, "a most difficult expedition."

Leo took a seat opposite him, eager now to hear what the newsman had to say about his travels. The prospects of a long, monotonous trip to Arizona Territory had begun to melt away with the presence of Henry Stanley to entertain them.

The engine let off steam and began to chug away from the depot as Stanley began to regale them.

"I was born in Denbigh, in North Wales, Dr. LeMat, so I am not a native American. I went to sea, to seek adventure. After sailing across several oceans and visiting many exciting countries, I came to America."

Leo sipped his brandy snifter, attentive to what Stanley was saying. "Go on, Mr. Stanley. It sounds like you lived an exciting life very early."

Stanley tipped back his own brandy, then drew

deeply on his Cuban cigar. "After the Civil War, I went to Turkey and parts of Asia as a newspaper correspondent. Later, I became special correspondent for the *New York Herald*."

"But when did you enter Africa?" Leo asked as Jacques sat across the car looking on, listening as he drank his brandy from a chipped, stained coffee mug.

Stanley glanced at the ceiling for a moment. "I began my expedition to East Africa in 1871, eager to find Dr. David Livingstone if at all possible. There was a great deal of speculation here in America that he was dead. Dr. Livingstone went to central and southern Africa in 1840, with the hope of halting the slave trade. It was a very dangerous undertaking at the time, as I'm sure you'll agree, at the height of the slave ships coming to our coasts from Africa."

"Of course," Leo said, more attentive than ever now. As Stanley talked, he felt like he was visiting a part of world history first-hand.

"Livingstone combined geographical, religious, commercial, and humanitarian goals in his exploration. He seemed to fear nothing. After many months of wandering, lost in the African jungles, I finally located him on the northern end of Lake Tanganyika. He was seriously weakened by disease, and this is where he finally died in 1873."

"It must have been an arduous journey to reach him," Leo observed.

"Indeed. Fifty-two of my bearers and associates were so badly crippled with leg ulcers and malnutrition that I had to leave them on the riverbank at a place I named 'Starvation Camp.' We were all close to death from hunger and local diseases, not to mention weakened by the insects and snakes and other perils common to the African jungle."

Leo shook his head. "It would take more than a dash of backbone to attempt such a feat, Mr. Stanley. You have my respect and admiration."

Jacques noticed their empty glasses and dutifully got up to pour more brandy as the train swayed along desolate tracks toward Fort Worth, the fiery ball of sun now lowering in the west.

"Livingstone was the man with tremendous courage," Stanley said. "He entered uncharted territory without the slightest hesitation, to accomplish what he felt were worthwhile goals. He traveled up and down the Congo and Nile river systems without a map or any records to guide him."

"How tragic that it cost him his life," Leo observed while Jacques refilled their glasses.

"I saw a great deal of that country myself," Stanley explained. "After Dr. Livingstone died, I journeyed into central Africa to look for suitable colonies for Leopold II of Belgium. I navigated Victoria Nyanza, proving it to be the second largest freshwater lake in the world. I also had the good fortune to discover the Shimeeyu River, and I traced the Congo River to its source. It was a grand experience, but among the most difficult undertakings anyone could imagine."

Leo was fascinated, feeling fortunate to have met a man like Stanley. "I believe I also read that you were the first to make the complete voyage up and down the Ururi River, some eight hundred miles long, if my memory serves me well."

Stanley smiled. "It would seem you've read articles about my lecture tours, Dr. LeMat."

"So I have," Leo replied, leaning forward in his chair as the train clattered over uneven sections of track north of San Antonio. "However, I'm just as interested in why you would be headed for Tombstone to make the acquaintance of Marshal Wyatt Earp."

Stanley shrugged, puffing on his cigar. "Men who clearly demonstrate courage continue to fascinate me. I must admit I was fooled by Wild Bill Hickok. But I understand that Marshal Earp is every bit as good as his reputation. He seems almost invincible, according to the stories about him."

"So I have heard," Leo remarked, tossing back another mouthful of brandy. "This is the reason my associate and I are traveling to Tombstone. If he is, as reports indicate, an utterly fearless man, I want to capture him on canvas. I also under-

stand he has brothers, Morgan and Virgil, who
are as notorious as Wyatt seems to be."

Stanley chuckled as he tapped ash from his
cigar into an ashtray by his side. "Some of these
Wild West characters are little more than savages,
Dr. LeMat. They live in a harsh environment
where comparisons to a civilized society cannot
be made."

"*Oui*," Jacques said, wearing a sour expression.
"If there is any place on earth worse than Abilene,
or all of Kansas, I hope never to see it . . . although I fear this is our destination in Tombstone."

Stanley gave Leo a look of appraisal. "I have
described my exploits in minor detail, Dr. LeMat.
Now I ask you to tell me how a medical doctor
becomes both a painter of portraits and an executioner with a gun."

Leo watched the empty south Texas hills, thick
with stunted mesquite trees and cactus and yucca
spikes, pass by a coach window before he replied.
"I deny the brand you've given me as executioner, Mr. Stanley. I have, on occasion, used my
gun to take a man's life."

"On a number of occasions," Jacques muttered,
earning him a stern glance from Leo.

"I originally went East to study medicine, as
my father before me. I had the good fortune to
meet Mr. George Catlin, perhaps the greatest of
all portraitists in the country. I fiddled around

with painting, but never seriously, until one day when Mr. Catlin happened to see me sketching a young woman sitting in a park. At the time, I did not know who he was, except by reputation, of course."

"He approved of your artistry?" Stanley asked.

Leo nodded. "In fact, he appeared to be quite enthusiastic about it. He invited me to his studio."

"You were studying medicine at the time?"

"Indeed, and if the truth be known, I'd grown rather frustrated with it. My wife died giving birth to our daughter . . . the young woman you see in the portrait on the wall. There was nothing anyone could do to save her. I lost all faith in the field of medicine after she died."

"But your daughter survived?"

"Yes. She is in one of the best boarding schools in New Orleans. I see her as often as I can, but my heart is no longer in medicine. It's an inexact science, at best."

Stanley's brow furrowed. "You have explained your acquired talents at painting and medicine . . . but I'm still curious how a man like you becomes a shootist."

Leo grinned, yet the smile did not fully reach the black centers of his eyes. "I have a dark side, I suppose, a gift from my mother's side of the family."

"Please explain, Dr. LeMat. . . ."

"My mother is related to the infamous Younger brothers, a band of outlaws I'm sure you've heard of during their affiliation with Jesse James."

"Of course. Bob and Cole . . . and I believe there was another. They were all cousins, as I recall."

"It doesn't matter," Leo continued, watching the window again as the train sped north. "There are times when I cannot ignore a challenge, or turn my back when a wrong needs to be righted. Something changes deep inside me. I'm at a loss to explain it any further. It's a subject I rarely discuss with anyone, Mr. Stanley."

"But your uncle, François LeMat, patented this odd pistol you carry. Perhaps your violent tendencies come from both sides of your family."

Leo inhaled deeply on his cigar. "I never question it. Left alone, to my own devices, I'd prefer to paint portraits and live peacefully."

"Yet you seemed more than willing to shoot down Mr. Longley if he refused to obey your order to raise his hands."

Jacques let out a quiet chuckle. "This Bloody Bill Longley, whoever he may be, had no idea how close he was to joining his ancestors."

Stanley seemed bewildered, a blank expression on his face for a time. Then he fixed Leo with a look. "How many men have you killed with a gun, Dr. LeMat . . . if the question is not deemed too indelicate?"

"I don't count them," Leo said, turning his attention to his daughter's portrait. "It would be a meaningless number, if I kept a count, which I do not. Assigning a number to a man's life, as if he were no more than a marker to be tallied, is disrespectful. It's like notching one's pistol. It diminishes both the living and the dead."

Stanley looked to Jacques for an answer.

Jacques was careful with his reply, for he knew how much Leo disliked talking about his duels. "A dozen would be too few," he said softly. "A hundred is too many. Let us talk about far more pleasant things . . . even if we are bound for the gates of hell in Arizona. I hear it is so hot in Tombstone that chefs never bother to build a fire in their cookstoves. If they require an egg to be cooked for some recipe, they put a cast-iron skillet outside in the sun for no more than five minutes and then place the egg inside it. *Mon Dieu!* We travel through this miserable heat only to reach a place where it is even hotter."

Leo gave Jacques a wink. "You've been getting fat around the middle, *mon ami*. A few weeks in the Arizona heat will sweat off a few of your extra pounds."

Jacques got up to fill their snifters again. Leo directed his next remark to Henry Stanley. "Tell me what you know about the forthcoming excavations beneath the pyramids, Mr. Stanley. What do you expect they'll find?"

Stanley leaned back in his chair. The coach

swayed around a tight turn. "Riches beyond all men's dreams, Dr. LeMat. These giant wonders of the world were not built out of idleness. I am certain that beneath the pyramids, golden treasures we cannot yet comprehend will come to the surface. To pass the time, I'll tell you a story I heard from an Egyptian grave robber many years ago . . . it concerned a local superstition that there was a curse placed on all who would desecrate their graves by the Egyptian royalty centuries ago. . . ."

"A curse?" Jacques asked as he steadied the brandy bottle against the rocking motion of the coach and refilled Stanley's snifter.

"Yes, Jacques. You see, the Egyptian royalty feel that they cannot enter the afterlife—that's what they call what we think of as heaven—unless their bodies are intact. They also believe they will have access to all their worldly goods that are buried with them. Thus the pharaohs are all buried with gold and silver and jewels so they won't be poor in the afterlife."

"I would think the men who prepared the bodies and buried all that gold and silver would be sorely tempted to come back later and take it for themselves," Jacques said, sitting across from Stanley.

Stanley smiled, nodding. "I think you are right, Jacques. Perhaps that is why the men who prepare the tombs, with traps to catch the tomb robbers, have their tongues cut out so they cannot reveal the secrets of the pyramids to would-be robbers."

Jacques's face screwed up in distaste. "Their tongues are cut out?" he asked in disbelief, glancing at Leo. "These workers are treated even worse than I am by my boss, it seems," he said.

Leo laughed. "I'm sure for you, *mon ami*, having your tongue cut out to end your ceaseless chatter, would be a fate far worse than death."

Chapter 5

Just the mention of grave robbers and curses sent Leo's mind back into his childhood, to a time when he first befriended Jacques in New Orleans.

They had known each other only a couple of years. Leo was from a blue-blooded family living on Rue Royale, one of the finest, most expensive neighborhoods in the city. Jacques came from the wharf district, where day laborers and dock workers lived in crowded, ramshackle quarters amid some of the worst filth Leo had ever seen. Disease was rampant. The stench of garbage and rotting fish overwhelmed visitors in the dank heat of summer.

They were an unlikely pair, the offspring of a French-Cajun whore from the worst section of New Orleans's slums, and the son of one of the city's most prominent physicians. Leo attended private Catholic school. Jacques had no formal education, only native curiosity and unschooled intelligence about the world around him that seemed to Leo to be out of character for a product of the back streets where mere survival was difficult.

They met one night at the old Angeline cemetery after they became friends, for it was Leo's habit to slip out of his family's mansion after everyone was asleep to prowl places he was forbidden to go during the daylight hours. His curiosity about the dark underbelly of New Orleans kept him awake at night: the seedy characters, the inherent violence, and the mysteries of voodoo ceremonies conducted by torchlight in poorer parts of the city. Jacques and Leo had begun an uneasy association two years earlier, when Leo's expensive clothing drew a remark from a wiry twelve-year-old Cajun boy idling near a gaslight on Canal Street. A fight resulted, first with bare fists, and then with a stiletto Jacques carried in a boot. Despite Jacques's street-honed skills at fighting, Leo was able to best him and wrest his knife away from him, a curious beginning for a lasting friendship.

On this night at the cemetery, they were just beginning their planned exploration of the wharf front, when Jacques noticed five men breaking into a tomb below a Spanish moss-laden cypress tree near the center of the graveyard. A pale moon outlined the shapes of the grave robbers, and what they were doing.

"Look, *mon ami*. Those men are robbing a grave

for the rings and jewelry of the dead." Jacques said it in a matter-of-fact way, as though it meant nothing.

Leo peered through a rusting wrought-iron fence at the five dark silhouettes breaking into a marble crypt. The sounds of their iron tools invaded the eerie quiet of the cemetery.

"We should send for the police," Leo whispered, intent upon the robbers.

Jacques chuckled. "You *are* a sheltered one," he said in a low voice. "They may be policemen themselves. Grave robbing is so common here that hardly anyone notices. The burial chambers of the rich are easy pickings for men who need money, including the policemen of New Orleans when they are off duty."

Leo sighed. "Then we do nothing but watch?" he asked.

"I have tried to teach you the ways of the poor, the criminals, people of the night. You live in your big house with no fear of someone robbing you, or killing you while you sleep. Here, life is very different. Every dark corner, every alleyway, is a place where you can lose your life. There is no area where you are safe. You live by your wits, by not making foolish mistakes or turning your back on anyone, even the police."

Leo heard a metal hinge creak near the crypt. "There's no sanctity, even for the dead, it would seem."

"What would you have us do, *mon ami*? Do we risk our lives to stop thieves from robbing someone who is no longer one of the living? The dead man doesn't care."

"I find it hard to ignore, Jacques. Watching it happening now makes me sick to my stomach. Those men are lower than fly maggots . . . they are vermin of the lowest form. They deserve to join the sleeping corpses here."

Jacques merely shrugged. "They look for gold and silver and jewels. The dead no longer need them. I have seen them pick the gold out of dead men's teeth. To them, it is simply a matter of money."

"It sickens me," Leo said, gripping the fence rods with his hands. Inside his coat, tucked into the waistband of his pants underneath his shirt, he had one of his uncle's pistols. "If I could get away with it without facing murder charges, I'd shoot every one of the rotten sons of bitches."

"Shoot them?" Jacques asked, more curious than shocked.

"Yes. I'd put bullets through their brains."

"You would need a gun, *mon ami*."

"I have one."

Jacques let a silence pass. "You have one with you now?" he said.

"Yes. One of my uncle François's prototypes, a pistol with a middle barrel filled with buckshot."

Jacques wagged his head. "You have much to

learn, Leo. This is none of our affair. We are not being robbed. Let the thieves take whatever they can find. What difference does it make to you?"

"It's wrong."

"The world is filled with wrong things. Do you think you can change them all?"

"I could change this one . . . I could kill every one of the grave-robbing bastards."

"Have you ever killed a man?" Jacques asked after a moment of quiet.

"Of course not. But killing these grave robbers wouldn't interrupt my sleep."

Jacques stared at him for some time, saying nothing. "Let me see your pistol," he said.

Leo drew the Baby LeMat from his waistband. He handed it over to Jacques.

Jacques felt its heft, examining it closely, turning it over in his hands. "Tell me again, *mon ami*, and look me in the eye when you say it. Are you willing to risk everything, even your own life, to kill simple grave plunderers?"

"Yes. Without a doubt. Will you go with me?"

Jacques grinned, widening an old knife-wound scar down one cheek. "Of course, Leo. I have no gun, but my blade can end a man's life as surely as this revolver. Come with me. I'll show you a way through the fence. . . ."

At fourteen, Leo was already six feet tall, weighing close to one hundred and eighty pounds, larger than most fully grown men, with hardened muscles and a quick temper that his father insisted came from his mother's side of the family. As he and Jacques crept through a narrow opening in the iron bars at the back of the cemetery where someone had carefully cut them away, they could hear muted voices coming from the crypt.

Jacques halted Leo suddenly with a hand. "I hear a woman's voice," he whispered.

Leo listened closely. A deep woman's voice came from one of the shadowy forms standing near the open mausoleum door.

"Prepare the gris-gris," she said. "Draw the circle in chicken blood, to appease the spirits."

"What the hell's she talking about?" Leo asked softly.

"Voodoo." He peered around a marble headstone for a moment to get a better look. "I recognize the woman now. She is Marie Laveau, the Voodoo Queen over all of New Orleans. She is a very dangerous woman, Leo, and she has many followers. I think we should leave. Let them take what they want from this dead man. It will make us many enemies if we interfere with a Voodoo ceremony being conducted by Queen Laveau. She has too many friends in this city. No place will be safe for us if we are recognized."

"I don't give a damn who she is, Jacques. What they're doing is wrong."

Jacques sighed. "There are times when you have more courage than good sense, *mon ami*."

"Then I'll do it alone. I have nine shots in this revolver and there are only five of them."

"You would shoot the woman, the Queen of Voodoo, Marie Laveau?"

It was something he hadn't considered. "No. Not the woman, only the others."

Even in the dark, Leo could easily see the frown on Jacques's face. "If she lives she'll put a Voodoo curse on you and you could die a miserable death."

"I don't believe in curses, or in Voodoo," he replied in a low whisper. "Either come with me, or stay behind."

Jacques wiped the gleaming blade of his dagger on a ragged shirt sleeve. "I will come around from the other side of the crypt," he said. "You have yet to learn how to place your heavy feet down so they don't make enough noise to awaken the dead."

Jacques disappeared into the deep shadows of the cypress trees, moving from gravestone to gravestone without making a sound.

When enough time had passed to allow Jacques to circle the crypt, Leo came to a crouch with his pistol aimed in front of him and began a slow approach toward the grave robbers.

He'd only taken a few steps when the shape he

now recognized as Marie Laveau turned toward him.

"Who goes there?" she demanded, her coarse voice almost masculine.

Leo halted fifty feet away. "Someone who intends to stop you from robbing a dead body," he said. "I have a gun, and I give you my word I'll kill every one of you unless you leave this place now."

The heavy-bodied woman put her hands on her ample hips, but it was the movement made by one of the others, a slender man in a dark coat, that held Leo's attention. He was reaching for something inside his belt.

"Don't do it!" Leo warned, turning the barrel of his LeMat toward the man. He could not possibly miss at this range.

His warning was ignored. The flash of gun metal appeared in the slender man's hand. Without a moment's hesitation, Leo pulled the trigger.

The blast of a forty-four caliber bullet split the eerie silence blanketing the graveyard. The man with the pistol was lifted off his feet, twirling, tossing his weapon into the dark grass as he slumped to the ground before the echo of the gunshot faded.

Leo saw the woman stiffen, but she did not run or make any effort to hide. "Shall I kill another of your associates, Madame, or is one enough?" he asked, feeling blood rush through his veins making his heart hammer and his mouth turn dry.

"You are a fool!" Queen Laveau snapped. "Do you know who I am? I can have you killed before the sun goes down tomorrow."

"I know who you are, Madame Laveau," he told her, as the man on the ground twisted and groaned. "Having me killed may be a bit more difficult than you think, but you have my invitation to try it whenever it suits you."

This further angered the Voodoo Queen. She glanced at yet another of her accomplices. "Kill him, Andre! Shoot him now! I command it!"

Andre reached into a pocket of his loose-fitting pants, when a fleeting silhouette leapt up behind him. Then Andre's head flew back when a fist seized his hair, and a glittering knife passed across his throat so quickly it was difficult to see.

"Arrgh!" Andre gurgled as he sank to his knees with Jacques standing behind him, his knife dripping blood.

Andre made one more gurgling sound before he fell over on his face, both feet twitching with death throes.

And now Marie Laveau appeared to shrink away from Jacques and Leo, stepping back from the open door of the tomb. Her two surviving companions gave Jacques a wide berth as they made to follow her. Leo did not fear the mulatto woman's threats—his gun sights remained on the men with her.

"Who are you?" she cried angrily.

Leo stepped closer to her, allowing her a glimpse of his face in spite of the darkness, anger and adrenaline still throbbing in his chest. "I am the breaker of Voodoo spells, the protector of the dead." He recalled something he'd read in Catholic school. "I am the anti-Christ. I've come to New Orleans parish to rid this city of Voodoo witches and grave robbers. If one more grave is robbed in New Orleans, I'll come looking for you, Madame Laveau. You cannot hide from me. Your spells have no effect on me, for I am the son of Beelzebub, a disciple of Satan sent to destroy all who violate the corpses of the dead. Pay close heed to my warning or I'll place your severed head on a pointed stake in front of the cemetery for all to see. Now go, before I decide to cut off your head tonight!"

The Voodoo Queen and her men backed farther into the darkness. The blackness wrapped its arms around her and she melted into it, disappearing as if it had consumed her.

The man Leo shot let out a final groan and lay still as Jacques walked up. For some odd reason, Jacques was grinning.

"The anti-Christ?" he asked Leo. "And who the hell is this Beelzebub? A disciple of Satan, indeed.

Mon Dieu! Where do you come up with these wild things?"

"I'll explain later," Leo promised, putting his still-warm pistol into his waistband. "Let's get the hell out of here before the gunshot brings the police, or a caretaker."

Jacques was still chuckling softly as they made their way toward the hole in the fence. "Beelzebub," he muttered over and over again. "There is a touch of utter madness inside your head, my friend. And now, you have killed a man. . . ."

As they bent to scramble through the fence, a woman's bloodcurdling scream came from the darkness, followed by an incantation in French: *"Je serai de retour, le garçon blanc, et ce sera le jour le plus noir de votre vie!"*

Hurrying through to the other side, Leo glanced at Jacques. "What'd she say?" he asked. "I didn't understand. . . ." He shivered as a cold, gray tendril of fog surrounded them as if mournful ghosts were reaching to caress them.

"She said she would be back, white boy, and it will be the blackest day of your life."

He would remember that night years later when he stood in a steady drizzle at the funeral of his wife. He looked up from the casket being lowered into the ground and saw a white-haired mulatto female standing next to a gravestone a short distance away. She was holding a small rag doll, and she was smiling and nodding, as if an old debt had been repaid. Leo blinked to clear the rain from his eyes, and she was gone, though there was no place to hide in the cemetery.

Devastated by the death of his wife in child-birth, and by his inability to save her even though he used all of the medical knowledge at his disposal, Leo was consumed by guilt at the thought that perhaps a youthful indiscretion had contributed to the death of his loved one.

It was this guilt that caused him to give up the practice of medicine, a profession he'd spent years of his life preparing for. The one consolation he had was his love of painting.

He closed his medical practice and turned his attention to his art, becoming within a few years one of the foremost portraitists in New Orleans.

However, his art alone was not enough to satisfy and keep at bay the demons in his soul, his so-called dark side. When he became aware of his unique ability with a gun, he decided to put his proficiency to good use and began to advertise his willingness to hire his to those who needed it.

He made sure to only take on clients who deserved his help, men and women who by their very nature were ill equipped to fight back when they'd been wronged or taken advantage of. Most of the time he'd been able to help them without even drawing his gun, such was his reputation and skill. Oftentimes he would work for free if the client had little money, only doing what he could to help right wrongs or set things right.

The feelings he experienced when he was able to help those less fortunate, did a great deal to fill the emptiness left in his soul by the death of his wife. In his mind, helping others less fortunate than himself was his way of showing thanks for the blessings of his life, blessings he didn't always think he deserved.

Chapter 6

Tucson was a beehive of activity, resting on a flat plain where a major wagon road to southern California crossed the dry plains west of New Mexico Territory. After crossing hundreds of desert and mountainous miles from Fort Worth, even the pleasant company of Henry Stanley and his tales of his world travels and explorations had grown tiring for Leo and Jacques. For days they watched the scenery through coach windows, lulled by the chug of the locomotive, a sound broken only by stops for water and coal, and to take on bare essential food supplies that would not perish in the late fall heat, since ice for the icebox would melt in only a few hours.

The sun, white-hot and blistering, seemed to suck the very life out of the landscape. What vegetation managed to survive was dry and scaly, stunted and misshapen, and usually covered with thorns. Jacques said even the air smelled like an overdone soufflé . . . dry and scorched.

When the train finally labored into Tucson it was a welcome relief from the monotony of the view, though not from the heat.

"I will make arrangements to have the coach parked on a side railing," Jacques said as they climbed down, stiff-kneed. "While the two of you find us a suitable place to eat, if such a thing exists in this wasteland, I will also see about hiring a surrey to take us to Tombstone."

"I'm sure there is a stagecoach line down to Tombstone," Stanley said, brushing soot and cinders from the locomotive off of his coat, shirtfront and straw hat.

Jacques turned up his nose, answering for Leo as well as himself. "Stagecoaches have the roughest ride on earth. We would all be sick by the time we got there . . . if we got there at all, since highwaymen use stagecoaches as one of their favorite targets. It is in all the newspapers. News of stagecoach robberies out here are as common as houseflies at a fish market."

Leo gave the downtown section of Tucson a glance. "Mr. Stanley and I'll look for something edible in reasonably comfortable surroundings. See to the coach, Jacques. We'll get our luggage later when we find a suitable conveyance to take us to Tombstone. And make sure all the padlocks on the doors and luggage compartments are securely fastened. I've already seen more than enough to convince me this town's full of unsavory types."

Stanley nodded. "Yes. It looks like almost everyone is carrying a gun of some description."

Leo laughed, placing his hand on Stanley's shoulder, leading him toward the downtown streets. "Don't let that bother you, Mr. Stanley. In the West, guns are like pants. Everyone wears them because they're expected to. But it doesn't mean they all know how to use them."

Jacques wiped sweat off his face with a forearm. "This may turn out to be even worse than Kansas, Leo. We should not have come until it got cooler. A block of ice would bring a king's ransom in this furnace of a town . . . and there's enough dust in the air to make bricks, if we only had water and straw. In spite of what you have told me about the earth being round, this town may prove you wrong. This may be the very end of civilization, and if it is not, it is surely the last place God made. I wish we had stayed in San Antonio."

Leo and Stanley ambled off toward the center of town while Jacques made for the railroad depot office, grumbling all the way.

"Your friend," Stanley observed dryly, "is a strange fellow. On the one hand he seems more than capable of fending for himself against virtually any obstacle, while he continually complains about conditions. He is obviously quite a rugged individual, yet he is clearly unhappy to be here."

Leo chuckled, working the kinks out of his knees as they walked. He could see a sign above the Blue Diamond Saloon a few blocks away. "It's his nature to complain, Mr. Stanley. But no one I've ever met has endured more hardships than Jacques. Pay no attention to him. He grew up in one of the roughest parts of New Orleans, a street urchin. This is only his way of letting off steam."

"He showed me his shotgun," Stanley remembered. "A deadly piece if I've ever seen one. He would only need to stand a few yards away to destroy everything or everyone in front of him. I surmise it has one hell of a kick. And I've seen him sharpening his knife on a whetstone while the two of us were talking. He does it with a certain fascination . . . much the same as when he oils his sawed-off shotgun."

"He shortened it himself many years ago, when most of the fights he found himself in were at very close quarters. But you are correct to assume that his ten-gauge is quite deadly. He has proven it a number of times. And when it comes to handling a knife, I've seen few who were his equal. But on the whole he is a very gentle man who prides himself on his cooking, not his facility with weapons. Over the years he has put the violent part of his past behind him, for the most part."

Moving up the street, Leo was distracted by the

appearance of a mounted army patrol moving at a trot through the center of town.

"I wonder what this is all about?" Stanley said, thinking the same as Leo.

Leo spotted a dapper gentleman in a derby hat and brown suit with a badge pinned to his vest, standing in the shade of a porch watching the cavalry patrol pass by. Leo surmised someone in authority would know why the soldiers were moving through the otherwise quiet town.

"Excuse me, sir," Leo began, "but we just got off the train and we were wondering about the cavalrymen. Is this something unusual?"

The man wearing a constable's badge gave Leo a quick look of appraisal. "It's Geronimo," he replied tonelessly.

"Geronimo, the Apache?" Stanley asked.

The constable nodded. "He's escaped from the San Carlos reservation again. Maybe fifteen or twenty warriors and a handful of women are reported to be with him. The army has been called out to bring him back."

Leo had read a great deal about Geronimo and his fierce determination to wage war against the white man. "There must be eighty soldiers in that column," he said as clouds of alkali dust arose from the cavalry horses' heels.

The constable replied softly, knowingly, "It'll take that many an' maybe a helluva lot more to catch him this time. Word is he's headed into the

Dragoons toward Tombstone, movin' toward Mexico, where he's safe from the army."

Stanley gave Leo a worried look. "We are bound in that same direction, Dr. LeMat. Perhaps we should spend a few days here in Tucson until the army catches the Apaches. Our journey might be safer."

The constable chuckled before Leo could reply. "Don't worry none. This bunch of green recruits under Cap'n Baker couldn't catch up to Geronimo in a thousand years. Fort Thomas is full of new recruits who barely know how to saddle a horse. Geronimo is probably laughin' all the way to the Mexican border. They'll never catch sight of him. He's deep in those Catalina Mountains by now, and even with the best Indian scouts the army's got, they won't find a single track."

"I understand they call him the Human Tiger," Stanley went on.

"Sounds pretty damn close to the truth. He's escaped half a dozen times. The army was gonna hang him the last time, until General Crook intervened. Can't imagine why Crook would feel sorry for a bloody savage like Geronimo, but it's real plain he did."

Leo watched the columns of soldiers head south across the railroad tracks out of town. Off in the distance, barren rock mountains loomed against a clear late-morning sky. He thought, but did not say, how much he desired the opportunity to paint the famous Apache war leader, knowing it was about as unlikely a possibility as he could imagine.

He spoke to the constable. "Thanks for your information, sir. Can you direct us to a good place to eat and a hotel with decent rooms and a bathhouse?"

"The Palace has got both—good food in the café an' clean rooms with a bathhouse out back. It's the best in town, if you are the picky type."

"We're obliged," Leo said, leading Stanley away from the porch toward a distant three-story building where a sign above the doors advertised "The Palace Hotel. Fine Food."

"Just our luck," Stanley muttered as they trudged through the heat and dust. "We arrive just in time to witness an Apache uprising."

Leo grinned. "One Indian with a dozen warriors trying to flee to Mexico won't pose a threat to us . . . not with the cavalry close at their heels."

"I'm still wondering if we should wait for a few days, until the renegades are caught."

"You heard what the constable told us. It isn't likely the army will catch him before he crosses the Mexican border. No need to delay our arrival in Tombstone any longer than absolutely necessary. After the Earp brothers' difficulties at the O.K. Corral, time may be of the essence. Someone with a grudge on the other side might shoot Marshal Earp in the back, before you get a chance to interview him and I to paint him." Leo grinned crookedly. "Bad for us, worse for him."

"This is *not* fish," Jacques said, chewing a forkful of food with a deep scowl on his face. "A skunk, perhaps, but not any kind of fish I've ever tasted."

Leo cut into his steak, finding it reasonably tender with a good flavor. "Any man without the good sense to avoid ordering seafood when he's a thousand miles from the closest ocean or river deserves whatever he gets," he said, enjoying his meal, as was Stanley.

"They described it as brook trout in lemon butter," Jacques complained bitterly. "So far, all I can find are fish bones and rotten rinds."

"In order to have brook trout as an offering, one must first have a brook in which the trout lives. It's simple deduction, my Cajun friend. For hundreds of miles we've seen no brooks or creeks, or even puddles large enough to support a population of fish. It's times like these when I wonder if your mother dropped you on your head when you were very young, inflicting serious brain damage."

Jacques tossed his fork onto his plate, a signal that he was giving up on his meal. "I cannot eat it. This is unfit for consumption by a member of the human race."

"This steak is delicious," Leo said, to further

prod Jacques into irritation. "When I suggested the steak, you said the cows we'd seen from our Pullman car windows were too thin to provide chewable meat. You were quite wrong, however.

Stanley gave them both brief, worried looks, not quite sure if this were friendly teasing, or a more serious matter between two friends.

"I would rather starve than eat this," Jacques said with a note of finality.

Leo looked out a window, feigning deep thought. "Some of life's most important lessons are learned at the brink of a man's grave. Where shall I send your personal effects?"

Jacques emptied his third glass of white wine. "Your sense of humor does nothing for the hollow spot in my gullet, Leo. I knew we should have stayed in San Antonio. Whoever this Marshal Wyatt Earp may be, he cannot be worth this much suffering. And now you tell me that we may be facing hostile Indians along the road to Tombstone."

"Only a few escaped from San Carlos," Leo reminded him. "They are being chased by almost a hundred mounted cavalrymen. We'll never see them. Geronimo and his band are fugitives. They won't bother a half-starved Cajun with no meat on his bones."

"Are Apaches cannibals?" Jacques asked, suddenly serious.

"No," Stanley replied. "The only known cannibals in North America were a tribe of south Texas Indians called Karankawas, and they no longer exist."

Jacques seemed uncertain, and Leo was enjoying his friend's discomfort. "Apaches merely take human scalps, *mon ami*. They cut off a portion of your hair and leave you alive to slowly bleed to death."

Jacques ran fingers through his hair unconsciously. "They will have to survive a kiss from my sweet Ange before they do," he said.

"Ange?" Stanley asked, halting a fork laden with fried potatoes near his mouth.

Leo gave the newsman his answer. "Jacques's given his shotgun a name. He sleeps with it at night, the way most men sleep with a woman, cradling it in his arms."

"Enough," Jacques said, pushing back his chair. "I will go down to the depot and see to the preparations for tonight. I have hired a surrey. The driver said he would meet us at six o'clock tomorrow morning beside the station. He warned me that the drive to Tombstone would take four or five hours, if we have no unforeseen delays."

"I've arranged for rooms here at the Palace for the night," Leo said. "Have someone bring our trunks to the hotel. We'll load the rest of our supplies early tomorrow morning, including my easel and oils."

"*Oui, certainement,*" Jacques replied, stalking

out of the café after he gave his uneaten platter of trout a final glare.

When Jacques was out on the street, Stanley spoke to Leo. "That is a deep scar on his face, a terrible disfigurement, if I may say so privately."

"A knife wound. He was ten years old when a Spanish seaman taunted him over his mother's . . . profession."

"Her profession?"

"She was a prostitute. A wharf-front whore. Her husband left her and the boy to fend for themselves when he was only nine."

"Jacques was fortunate he wasn't killed."

"On the contrary. Jacques killed the Spanish sailor with a knife and dumped his body in the river . . . though he later said he doubted if even the alligators in the swamps would stoop so low as to eat a Spaniard."

Stanley merely shook his head and chewed on his potatoes. "He seems a man of immense contradictions," he said.

"How so?" asked Leo.

"On the one hand, he seems more than ready to resort to violence, with his shotgun and knife, at the least provocation. On the other, he is a master chef and seems quite gentle most of the time."

Leo laughed. "Oh, Jacques *is* quite gentle. You should see him with children. He is like a genial grandfather to anyone younger than himself. He only resorts to violence when he, or someone he loves or respects, is threatened. But once the need for violence is over, he reverts back to a simple soul, content to use his skills in the culinary arts to provide sumptuous meals to please the palate."

Stanley nodded. "As I said, a man of contradictions."

Chapter 7

A gray-whiskered buggy driver introduced himself as Clifford Barnes. A two-seater carriage with a dusty black canvas top drawn by two thin bay harness horses waited for them beside the depot shortly after dawn. Jacques had eaten breakfast early enough to walk to the depot to prepare their luggage and gear for loading before Leo saw to the transport of their overnight bags from the hotel. He conceded that not even the cook at the Palace had been able to ruin scrambled eggs and bacon.

Rooms at the Palace had been adequate, although rather small in Leo's experience, and all three men agreed they'd spent a restful night after so many days fighting the heat and soot of a moving train.

Barnes gave the assortment of trunks and valises a doubtful look while Jacques was loading them in the back. "Ain't sure all that's gonna fit," he said, a cheekful of chewing tobacco making his

words mushy. "Only got the two harness horses."
He gave Leo's easel a narrow-eyed stare. "What
the hell is that there contraption?"

"A painter's easel," Leo replied.

Barnes spat in the dust and turned away from
the loading, saying, "I oughta charge you fellers
extra fer haulin' all this stuff so far."

Leo reached inside his coat. "Here's an extra
five dollars for you, Mr. Barnes. We wouldn't
want to put you or your horses through any hard-
ship."

Barnes quickly snatched the money, giving Leo
a yellow-toothed grin. "I appreciate it, Doc
LeMat. I'll be real careful not to hit no bumps too
hard."

Stanley spoke to the driver, his concerns over
Geronimo having troubled him all night. "The
runaway Apache, Geronimo. Do you anticipate
that we might have any sort of difficulties with
him along the way?"

"Naw. Ol' Geronimo is smart. He knows them
soldiers is after him. If I was to take a guess, I'd
say he's already in the Dragoons by now."

"That's quite a relief," Stanley sighed, putting
the last of his carpetbag valises into the rear compartment, noticing that Jacques carried his
Greener shotgun over his shoulder on a worn
leather strap.

Jacques spoke to Leo. "It is all ready. The coach
is locked and everything is secured. As you can

see, I tied your easel to the rear of the canopy where it should make the trip without any damage."

Leo nodded, turning to Barnes. "We're ready, Mr. Barnes. Let's get under way before it gets any hotter."

Barnes climbed into the front seat. Jacques sat up front beside the driver while Leo and Stanley took their seats in the rear.

The carriage lurched away from the rail siding where Leo's coach was parked. Amid the rattle of harness chains and the clatter of iron-rimmed wheels over hard ground, Barnes swung his carriage and team southeast, toward Tombstone.

"Them's the Catalinas," Barnes replied to Leo's question as they skirted one rocky peak after another, following a wagon road with hardly any freighter traffic at this early hour. "Off yonder, to the south, is the Dragoons. Rough, empty sons of bitches with no roads. That'll be where ol' Geronimo is now, most likely."

"This is the driest land I have ever seen," Jacques said, a squint pinching his angular features in spite of the canopy shading his eyes. "How the hell does an animal find a damn thing to eat out here?"

"Oh, there's plenty of grass in places," Barnes replied, "only you gotta know where to look fer it. Wild game, or a Texas longhorn, they find it."

"How about water?" Stanley asked.

"Same thing. There's plenty of springs up in the mountains if you know where to look. Apaches know. This has been their land fer hundreds of years, only the white man came along an' took it away from 'em."

"They had it coming," Jacques muttered, watching every high nook and cranny in the surrounding mountains as though he expected to see Indians pouring out of the rocks at any moment. "They scalp people."

Barnes shrugged. "It's their way of doin' things. Hard to change a man's regular habits, even if he is a goddamn murderin' redskin."

Jacques face turned hard. "If you intend to kill a man with a knife, you cut out his heart and hand it to him while it's still beating. It's a stupid practice, to cut off the top of a man's scalp so he bleeds to death."

Barnes gave Jacques a sideways glance before he returned his attention to the road in front of them. "That ain't all they cut off, mister, in case you ain't heard. They take an enemy an' stretch him out in the sun by rawhide strips tied to stakes, an' then they cut off his eyelids so his eyeballs will boil in the sun. They'll tie him over a red ant bed if'n they can find one, so the ants can eat him real slow."

The muscles in Jacques's cheeks tightened. "If any of the bastards come after us, I will introduce them to the fiery touch of death from my sweet Ange." He gave the stock of his Greener a gentle kiss.

Barnes wagged his head and said nothing, clucking to his team as the carriage bumped over empty roadway. Stanley took out his handkerchief and mopped his sweating brow.

Leo decided to change the subject. "Mr. Barnes, what have you heard about this shooting at a place called the O.K. Corral in Tombstone?"

The driver seemed to hesitate before he gave his answer. "I don't reckon it's over, if that's what you mean. The Earp boys an' Doc Holliday shot the hell outta the Clantons an' McLaurys last month. Killed three of 'em."

"What makes you say it isn't over?"

"Some of the worst of that bunch . . . they call themselves the cowboys, are still on the loose. Word's all over this part of the territory they's plannin' revenge against them Earps afore too long."

"Who're these remaining cowboys? I believe I've read about some of them," Leo asked.

Another pause while Barnes appeared to be thinking. "Johnny Ringo's the worst. A natural-born killer. Curly Bill Brocius is another who's nearly as bad. Then there's Ike Clanton an' a bunch more who'll be after the Earp brothers. Like I said, nobody figures it's over just yet . . . not so long as Ringo an' Curly Bill are alive."

"But aren't the Earps duly authorized peace officers?" Leo persisted.

Barnes chuckled. "That don't amount to a hill o' shit in this neck o' the woods, Doc. A badge ain't gonna stop no bullet in Cochise County."

"Why won't the army intercede?"

"Some say they will. There's an inquiry bein' held by the commanding officer up at Fort Grant, but nobody expects it to amount to much. There's a helluva lot of local politics involved in this. It ain't my place to say it, but them Earps may have bit off more'n they can chew."

"Do you know any of the Earps personally?" Leo continued, for it was frequent to find local opinion very different from the man or his actions.

"I've played some monte at the Oriental while Wyatt was dealin' the cards."

"What's your impression of him, if you don't mind having me ask?"

"One tough son of a bitch. He ain't afraid of no man I ever saw. Fearless as hell if somebody challenges him, an' he damn sure ain't bashful about usin' his guns."

"I take it he's good with a pistol," Stanley piped in.

Barnes required more time to reply. "He ain't what I'd call a quick-draw artist, like Doc Holliday. Holliday's as fast as Ringo, an' Ringo knows it. I figure that's one reason why Ringo didn't take a hand in the shootin' at the O.K. Corral. But Doc is dyin' of lung disease, an' he's real bad about gettin' drunk at night."

"Tuberculosis?"

"Never heard what it's called, but he spits up blood sometimes an' his color don't look just right. Pale as a damn ghost, an' his skin looks like leather that's been left out in the sun too long . . . kinda yeller like."

Leo digested what the driver was telling them. He needed to know as much as he could about his subject before the portrait was begun, for sometimes the inner man could be shown in a subject's eyes.

Stanley wiped his brow again. "I hope Marshal Earp and his brothers will grant me an interview for my story," he said. "I sent him a telegram, but received no reply. I fear it may have arrived during this bloody killing spree, thus I shouldn't wonder why he didn't send me an answer."

"He ain't the real talkative type," Barnes offered. "Now an' then when he's at the Oriental, he'll loosen up some, but don't mistake that for bein' friendly. He owns part of the game an' it's just business to him."

The passengers and driver settled into a silence as slow miles passed beneath the buggy wheels. The air was hot and dry and dusty, and carried no scent other than sweating horses and warm leather.

* * *

Buzzards circling in the air announced trouble long before they crested a hill in the desert flats south of the Catalina range. Dozens of vultures circled a particular spot near a stand of brush near the road.

"A covered wagon," Jacques said when they rolled over the ridge.

"And no horses or mules tied to the tongue," Leo added as he took in every detail.

The road had been empty for hours. The wagon was the first vehicle they had seen in some time.

"Somebody's dead up yonder," Barnes declared, pulling back on the reins. "Maybe more'n one. Sure as hell are a bunch of them birds circlin'."

"I see a woman in a yellow dress," Jacques said. "She's lying behind the wagon."

Barnes held his team in check while they all studied the scene below.

"Goddamn Apaches," Barnes said finally. "Appears they jumped a bunch of settlers an' stole their livestock an' food. Looks like Geronimo ain't as close to Mexico as I figured he'd be."

Jacques flipped open the double barrel Greener to check its loads, then he pulled up his shirt where the butt of his pistol showed above his waistband. "I have never killed an Apache," he said softly. "Today, that might change."

"They'll be gone by now," Barnes insisted.

"One thing 'bout Geronimo . . . when he strikes, he does it quick an' then gets the hell outta there."

"Drive us down, Mr. Barnes," Leo said. "Perhaps there's something we can do for the survivors . . . if indeed there are any still living."

Four bodies lay in mottled shade beneath saguaro cactus, and green-backed blowflies swarmed over them in great, hovering black clouds. The stench of death, a coppery scent of blood and excrement mixed with the acrid smell of cordite, hung over the area like a miasma from a swamp.

Jacques bent over the body of a young woman, a girl in a tattered yellow dress that was now covered with dark stains, barely covering her bloodied loins. "They cut off her hair right down to the bone," he said as he moved the remnants of her dress to cover her nudity, his voice revealing a trace of emotion Leo had not heard from him in a number of years. Jacques had been witness to murder in almost every form, including the remains of men tossed into the bayous as food for alligators.

"They're all dead," Leo said as sounds of a heavy wagon drew closer from the southeast. The crack of a teamster's whip was almost lost to the creak of overloaded wagon axles and the clank of harness chains.

"Makes a man belly-sick," Barnes said, turning away from the sight of three other mutilated bodies lying nearby. One of the settlers was tied in a sitting position with his back to a wagon wheel, a small pile of still-smoldering coals in his crotch sending the smell of burning flesh across the desert.

Henry Stanley stood in the shadow of a saguaro examining the carnage. "Unbelievable," he mumbled. "We think we live in a civilized country. General Sherman may have been right to say we are justified in the utter extermination of all the Indian races in America."

Leo shook his head. "I'm not so sure of such things, Mr. Stanley. One cannot blame a wolf for attacking a sheep, nor a rattlesnake for trying to bite. It's in their nature to do such things." He shrugged. "And, as terrible as it is to our sensibilities, it may be no different for the Apache."

Barnes stalked back to his carriage. "Those folks had the bad luck to be in the same spot as Geronimo," he said. "This ain't the first time he's killed women an' children. All he cares about is gettin' to Mexico."

"But why did he kill these apparently innocent people?" Stanley asked.

"They had mules. Maybe some flour an' sugar."

"Mules?"

Barnes nodded before he climbed back in the seat of his buggy. "Mule meat is an Apache's favorite, now that there ain't no buffalo. Geronimo an' his bunch will load whatever they stole from those folks on the backs of their mules. Soon as them Apaches git hungry, they'll kill the mules an' roast 'em. I hear tell sometimes they eat the meat raw."

Jacques selected a poor moment to inject a note of grim humor into what they'd found on the road to Tombstone. "Raw mule meat could hardly be any worse than the trout at the Palace in Tucson."

Leo turned away. "We'll notify the authorities in Tombstone as to what we found. Let's tell the driver of that freight wagon to inform the army at Fort Grant."

Jacques was the last to board the carriage before Barnes drove away. "I am looking forward to my first chance to kill an Apache," he said, resting the butt plate of the Greener atop his knee. "I can already tell both Ange and I will enjoy it."

Chapter 8

When Leo and the other passengers in Clifford Barnes's carriage first set eyes on Tombstone, it appeared to be nothing more than a dust-blown collection of tents and shanties perched on a high plateau between the Dragoon and Whetstone mountains. A winding road from Tucson brought them within sight of the town in less than six hours of hot, monotonous travel. Although no one could forget the carnage they'd found west of the road, where the settlers lay mutilated beside their wagon, no one mentioned it again until they neared the city. It was enough to remember what the disfigured bodies looked like.

"Them's the San Pedro Hills," Barnes informed them as his carriage rattled up a slight incline leading to town. "Silver come pourin' out of them hills back in seventy-nine an' before you know it, Tombstone went from an empty flat to a city of damn near six thousand folks . . . most of 'em miners, of course, and them what deals in the trades sought by miners, if you know what I mean. This was all Apache country back then, until the army finally corralled 'em on the reservations. Now it's a place for sin peddlers and miners. A man can buy nearly anything he wants here in Tombstone."

"You mean whiskey, whores, and gambling," Stanley said as his eyes roamed the outskirts of town. "I don't see much beyond gaming parlors and whorehouses."

"Main Street's full of shops that sell prospectin' tools, an' damn near anything else a miner needs. There's still silver in them hills, only there's a helluva lot more men diggin' for it now."

"I see more substantial buildings farther into the city," Leo said. "Let's hope there's more to Tombstone than what we can see from here."

"There is," Barnes assured them. "Even got wooden boardwalks in front of the better places. They got two newspapers, the *Nugget* an' the *Epitaph*, along with an honest-to-goodness ice cream parlor right next to the Bird Cage Theater."

"A theater?" Jacques sounded surprised.

"Hell, that ain't all. Just this spring they opened up Julius Caesar's New York Coffee House, and a place called the Cosmopolitan Hotel."

"That sounds nice," Leo said, still watching the dusty plateau and its odd arrangement of buildings. "Is it truly a cosmopolitan place?"

"Nicest joint in town, Doc," Barnes said. "If I

was you, I'd hire me a room at the Cosmopolitan. Won't be near so many fights in that part of town, an' you won't be bothered by no batches of lewd women paradin' back an' forth in front of the hotel.

"Lewd women?" It was Jacques who asked.

"Whores," Barnes replied. "Tombstone's full of 'em, on account of all the miners with their pockets full of silver dust. Them miners stay up in the hills for weeks at a time collectin' their riches, an' when they come to town they's powerful hungry fer a woman."

Leo ignored Jacques's interest in prostitutes for the moment, leaning forward in the carriage seat. "Take us to the Cosmopolitan Hotel, Mr. Barnes, and then show us where the marshal's office is so we can report what happened to that family in the covered wagon."

"Won't do no good to report it," Barnes said, clucking to his team again. "But I'll take you to Marshal Earp's office so you can tell him what happened to them settlers. He'll tell you it's army business, but I reckon you need to hear that for your own self. We'll be drivin' right past the marshal's office on the way to the hotel."

They came to a shallow ditch at the outskirts of town filled with muddy water—an open sewer, Leo supposed, when his attention was drawn to a man with a bullwhip standing behind a team of lathered mules hitched to a wagon loaded with beer kegs. The mules were obviously refusing to cross the thin stream of water, but it was what the man with the whip was doing to the animals that caught Leo's notice.

Blood oozed from the flank of the off-hand mule where the blacksnake had left its mark. The mules' flanks were quivering as the barrel-chested man continued to flog them relentlessly over their refusal to cross the drainage ditch, even though it was only a few feet wide.

"Stop the buggy," Leo said when they came abreast of the man and his recalcitrant team.

Barnes looked over his shoulder, bewildered by Leo's firm request. "Why's that, Doc?"

"Stop the horses," Leo commanded again, stepping down from the carriage before it had come to a complete halt.

Leo walked up to the man with the bullwhip. Jacques slid quietly out of the front seat.

"What is he doing?" Stanley asked Barnes.

"I got no idea, mister," Barnes replied, still puzzled by the delay.

"Pardon me, sir," Leo began, his voice level, betraying no emotion. "I'm asking you to stop whipping these poor beasts. There's an easier way."

The beard-stubbled teamster gave Leo a cold stare. "Mind your own goddamn business, city slicker. I can tell by your fancy dress you don't know a damn thing about mules. Get back in your buggy an' clear out of here before I use this whip on you."

"I know when an animal is suffering needlessly. Take the time to lead one of them across. The other will follow it and you'll spare the useless whipping you're giving them. You're wasting your time using the whip."

"Them's my goddamn mules, you nosy son of a bitch. Git out of my way or I'll give you a taste of this rawhide. . . ."

No sooner had the words left the teamster's mouth than Leo swung a vicious backhand across the mule skinner's face, sending him flying backward until he landed on his rump.

The man wore a Colt .44 on his right hip, a risk Leo had already calculated.

"You bastard," the teamster hissed, glancing down at his holstered gun.

"Go ahead, my friend," Leo said, giving him a humorless smile. "Reach for your piece . . . if you have the nerve. I'll send you to an early grave."

The mule skinner raised up on his elbows. Blood trickled from one corner of his mouth. "You ain't even carryin' no gun, slicker. I'll kill you deader'n pig shit."

Leo's feigned grin widened briefly. "You're wrong on two counts," he said, still without inflection in his tone. "I am carrying a gun, and you'll be the one filling a six-foot hole if you're stupid enough to reach for your iron. But you may suit yourself on the matter . . . test your skill with that Colt, or get up and unhitch one of the mules."

A thick-fingered hand made a clawing motion toward the Colt.

Leo's gun came out of its shoulder holster in a well-practiced move before the teamster's fingers could close around the butt of his weapon.

The mule skinner froze, the whites of his eyes showing when he stared into the muzzle of the forty-four caliber LeMat in Leo's fist. He heard Leo cock his weapon, and when he heard the sound he drew in a breath.

"Bang," Leo said softly, hard to hear above noises coming from the edge of town. "You're dead to rights, just as I promised you'd be. The only thing missing is the bullet, and if you insist, I'll put one right between your eyes."

"Holy shit," the mule driver stammered.

"As far as I know, there's no such thing, although I'm not what you'd call a deeply religious man. Now get up and unhook a mule from the harness. Lead it across the ditch, then lead the other mule harnessed to the wagon and you'll be on your way again. I'm taking your bullwhip, since you seem incapable of knowing how and when to use it."

The driver sat up, rubbing his bleeding mouth.

"And one more thing," Leo continued. "If I ever see you whipping a mule again, for any reason, you have my word I'll shove that bullwhip up your ass before I kill you."

"Them's my mules," the teamster said again, struggling to his feet. "You can't just go 'round tellin' a feller how to use his own damn mules."

Leo bent over and picked up the bullwhip, an eight-foot plaited latigo. "Perhaps not," he said, coiling the wicked piece of leather, "but until I meet a man who's able to stop me from handing out advice on the treatment of mules, I'll keep on with my present practice. And for good measure, so you'll know this is no idle jest, I'll give you a small taste of what you've given these poor animals. . . ."

He aimed for the man's left boot top, a stovepipe that reached all the way to his knees. With one swift motion Leo cracked the whip across the teamster's ankle, cutting through worn boot leather with a single slash of the whip's tassels.

"Shit! Shit! Shit!" the mule skinner cried, lifting his left leg to grab his foot, hopping a few steps on the other foot until he slumped back to the roadway, his face twisted in a mask of pain.

"I gave you fair warning," Leo reminded as a small crowd of onlookers had begun to gather near the ditch when they heard the man's cries. "Remember what I said. If I hear that one more stroke of a whip has been administered to this mule team, I'll come looking for you."

He wheeled toward the carriage, finding Jacques standing only a few yards away with his shotgun cradled. Henry Stanley sat in the rear carriage seat with his mouth agape, saying nothing as Leo stalked back to the buggy.

Clifford Barnes spat a stream of tobacco juice into the dust near one carriage wheel. "Sure glad I didn't have to put no whip on these horses," he mumbled before Leo and Jacques returned to their seats.

The carriage rolled easily across the ditch and started into town, when Leo noticed a well-dressed man in a suit coat and vest leaning on a silver-handled cane, watching them from the front porch of a drinking parlor. He was wearing a pair of nickel-plated pistols at his waist.

"Be real careful," Barnes said over his shoulder. "Don't start no trouble with that feller."

"And why is that?" Leo asked, admiring the man's tailored attire and black beaver felt hat.

"That there's Doc Holliday. Don't nobody in Tombstone mess with him. He's got a bullet wound in his ass from that O.K. Corral shootin' an' he ain't likely in the best of humor. . . ."

"Stop the buggy," Leo said, his second request for a halt before they reached the center of town.

"You could be makin' a mistake, Doc LeMat," Barnes warned as he drew back on the horses' reins. "Holliday ain't no man to fool with."

The man Barnes identified as Holliday touched

the brim of his Stetson when the vehicle rolled to a stop. He gave Leo a curious smile.

"I saw what you did to the mule driver," Holliday said. "I admire a man who won't tolerate the mistreatment of dumb animals for any reason."

His voice was low and soft, rounded by a thick southern accent made hoarse by too much whiskey and tobacco.

Leo swung down carefully, his gaze never leaving Holliday's as he walked over to the porch of the Oriental Saloon. "I'm Dr. Leo LeMat," he said, "and our driver informs me that you're Dr. Holliday."

"Seems like I'm famous these days," Holliday said, a hint of sarcasm in his voice. "Are you a medical doctor?"

"I am, although I no longer practice medicine. I'm a painter, a portraitist." He extended his palm to Holliday.

They shook, and Holliday continued to seem mildly amused. "For a doctor and a painter, you come out mighty quick with that pistol. I saw you draw down on the teamster. Are you as good with a surgeon's scalpel and a paintbrush?"

Leo noticed Holliday's pale complexion, and the slight tremor in his hands. "Some say I am."

"I need a good doctor," Holliday said. "Having my picture painted holds very little interest for me. But the horse doctor they have here in Tombstone has done nothing to relieve the pain or the

festering of a bullet wound I have in my hip. If
you're not on your way elsewhere, I would gladly
pay to have you take a look at it."

"I came to Tombstone to paint Marshal Wyatt
Earp, so I'll be staying for some time," Leo
replied. "I'd be glad to take a look at your
wound."

Holliday chuckled. "You intend to paint Wyatt?
I find that laughable . . . he's a dear friend, but as
ugly as a mud fence. Why anyone would come
here to paint Wyatt is a mystery to me."

"His fame as a peace officer makes him an interesting subject," Leo replied. "Newspapers all
over the country were full of accounts of the
shooting here, which I understand you also took
part in."

"I did. Like I said, Wyatt and I have been
friends for a number of years. When it became
clear he might face more trouble than he or his
brothers could handle alone, I offered my services
to them." He smiled. "My reward was a bullet
through my right buttock, with which I am suffering greatly. I would gladly pay your fee to ex-
amine it and perhaps have something prepared
for me at the apothecary shop."

Leo nodded. "We intend to stay at the Cosmopolitan Hotel. Come to my room within the
hour. My medical bag will be unpacked and I'll
see what I can do for you."

"I'd be grateful, Dr. LeMat. See you in an hour. I'll tell Wyatt you're in town."

"He's expecting me," Leo said, turning back for the carriage.

"Remember I warned you," Holliday said as Leo climbed to his seat. "Wyatt's downright ugly. You'll have your work cut out for you to make a pretty picture out of him." He chuckled softly as the carriage pulled away, then he started to cough.

Leo noticed Holliday's handkerchief, when he lowered it from his mouth, was stained scarlet.

Stanley's eyes followed the retreating figure of Doc Holliday. "He doesn't look like the ruffian he is portrayed as being," Stanley said. "In fact, he looks more like a gentleman than a noted shootist."

Leo shook his head. "In your travels, have you ever seen a coral snake, Henry?"

Stanley stared at Leo, his face puzzled. "Yes. Why do you ask?"

"The coral snake, with its colorful bands of red and yellow, looks more like a fine lady's necklace than a deadly killing machine." He cut his eyes to Doc Holliday. "If you get close enough to look into Doc Holliday's eyes, Henry, you will see much the same look as those of a serpent's. They are flat, black, and utterly without feeling. A moment ago, though Holliday was amiable and friendly on the surface, I had the sudden feeling I was looking into the eyes of a corpse."

Chapter 9

Leo was hanging clothes in a freestanding wardrobe in his room when he heard a knock on the door. Their rooms were on the second floor, with hardwood floors covered with Oriental rugs, and windows facing southwest to allow breezes to flow through the rooms, a welcome relief from the heat.

Jacques, in an adjoining room with a connecting door, came through to answer the knock.

A tall, slightly muscular man with a flowing handlebar mustache, dressed in a topcoat and stovepipe boots, stood in the hallway. A flat-brimmed hat was pulled low over his eyes. Beside him was Doc Holliday.

Leo saw Holliday and walked over to the door. "Come in, Dr. Holliday. We haven't quite finished unpacking, however my medical bag is beside the bed."

"I wanted you to meet Wyatt," Holliday said, "since he's the reason you came to Tombstone.

Wyatt, this is Dr. LeMat, the man I told you about who has a soft spot in his heart for mules. He's the gentleman who came all this way to paint your picture."

Earp extended a callused hand before he entered the room, paying particular attention to Leo's shoulder holster and gun, since Leo had removed his coat and hat to facilitate his unpacking at the Cosmopolitan.

"Please to meet you, Doc LeMat," Earp said in a gruff voice with a trace of whiskey on his breath. "Doc tells me you come out real fast with that shoulder gun."

Leo stepped back to allow them in. Jacques looked on from a spot beside the door. Earp was a tall, lean man whose dark tan and wrinkled skin made him seem older than his thirty-one years. His eyes were a deep blue, with tiny red veins in the whites that indicated to Leo he indulged frequently in drinking whiskey. He had a high forehead with prominent widow's peaks and a receding hairline. He was wearing a starched high collar over a boiled white shirt and a black frock coat that hung to his hips. His boots were polished and rose to his knees with his pants legs tucked inside.

"It seemed necessary," Leo explained, taking in Earp's hard features, already at work with ideas as to how to begin his portrait of the lawman.

"The mule skinner reached for his pistol and I was left with no choice."

"Understandable," Earp said, strolling into the room, his boots gleaming with bootblack, a Colt Peacemaker in a belt around his waist, a shiny badge pinned to his coat lapel. "Some gents have to learn the hard way when a man means what he says."

Holliday came in behind Earp, relying upon his cane to support the weight on his right leg. He was more of a gaunt figure than Leo remembered on their first meeting . . . slender to the point of malnutrition, showing the effects of his tuberculosis with muscle deterioration and loss of skin color. He was little more than a skeleton underneath his fine apparel, scarcely a hundred and thirty or forty pounds. He had prominent ears, which seemed to stick out even more due to the thinness of his face, but Leo doubted very much if anyone had ever dared to tease the gunman about his appearance.

Leo closed the door, then he pointed to Jacques. "This is my associate, Jacques LeDieux. He's been with me for years." He spoke to Holliday. "If you'll kindly remove your coat and guns, and then lower your pants, I'll take a look at the wound in your hip."

"A bullet hit him in the ass," Earp said dryly. "We figure it's 'cause he was runnin' away from the fight." Having said that, Earp laughed. Then he stuck a hand-rolled cigar into his mouth, although he did not light it.

Holliday ignored Earp's remark and hobbled over to the bed using his cane. He shucked his coat and pistol belt, then he unfastened his pants.

"Lie down on your stomach on the bed," Leo instructed, picking up his leather medical case. "I see it's been bandaged and I'll have to remove that first. I can give you a small dose of laudanum before I begin probing the bullet hole, if you wish."

"Hell yes," Holliday replied. "Give me plenty. I've been drinking since nine this morning, however, the whiskey does no real good. My ass still hurts, and it's all on account of Wyatt and his no-good kin."

"You could have stayed in bed," Earp remarked. "For all the good you did us, we'd have been better off. A man who gets shot in the ass has no way to explain his way out of it. You were runnin' the other way, only you weren't fast enough to outrun a lead slug."

"To hell with you, Wyatt," Doc said, a suggestion of a smile crossing his face. "The next time you face more trouble than you can handle, I'll do just that . . . I'll stay in bed and then attend your funeral." He coughed wetly and brought a handkerchief to his lips. The cloth was stained with old blood, a sign that Holliday's tuberculosis was in an advanced stage.

Leo gave Holliday a small purple glass vial after the good-natured banter ended and Holliday uncorked it, taking a healthy swallow. "I'm ready," he said, lowering his undershorts before he lay across the mattress. "It seems I must suffer the indignation of showing my bare rear to a total stranger in order to survive the bullet I took that was meant for Wyatt."

Before he started to remove the bandage, Leo saw angry red streaks leading away from the wound, a sure sign of blood poisoning. The area around the wound was raised and raw-looking, with some black areas near the entrance wound indicating possible early signs of gangrene.

As Leo gently probed the edges of the swollen area with his fingertips, he recalled an article in a medical magazine he'd read recently.

"Are you familiar with the *Lancet*, the British medical journal, Dr. Holliday?"

"Yes, but since you've had the opportunity to put your hands on my butt, a favor I grant to few women and absolutely no men, you may call me John, Leo."

Leo chuckled. "There was a recent article by an Austrian physician, Philip Ignatz Semmelweiss, concerning suppuration of wounds," Leo said as he turned and took a gleaming, razor-sharp scalpel from his medical bag. "Dr. Semmelweiss advocates draining wounds that show signs of infection. He states it cuts the mortality considerably."

Holliday glanced over his shoulder at the knife in Leo's hand, took another deep swig of the laudanum, and buried his face in the pillow on the bed. "Then go to it, Leo."

Leo stuck the point of the scalpel into the wound, placing a cloth over the hole so the pus that drained wouldn't run down his cheeks. A muffled grunt from Holliday was the only indication of pain he showed, though Leo knew it must have hurt like hell.

After a few moments, the pus was completely drained from the wound and Leo reapplied a thick bandage. Holliday sat up, a smile on his face that totally transformed his demeanor. "Well, I'll be damned! The pain's completely gone."

Leo nodded as he wiped his blade on the cloth. "Well, the relief will only be temporary. The suppuration will reform, but I'll have the apothecary mix up a preparation that will speed healing. I'll also have them make you up some syrup that will help you with that cough."

Holliday got to his feet and pulled up his pants. He stuck out his hand. "I'm much obliged to you, Leo. How much do I owe you?"

Leo shook his head. "Nothing, John. I'm glad I was able to be of help."

"Then I owe you and Jacques the best dinner in town. It's the least I can do."

Leo nodded with a smile.

Earp stood in the doorway as Holliday limped out into the hall. "I'm not so sure about this picture-paintin' thing," he said to Leo, scowling. "I may not have time. My brother Morgan is badly hurt . . . can't use his arm. An' Virgil has a bullet hole in his leg. There's still nearly a dozen of those cowboys who sent word they're out to get us. I've got to get Morgan out of town since he can't defend himself in the shape he's in, an' maybe Virgil too. Then I've got to find a man named Ringo, an' another son of a bitch named Curly Bill. Ike Clanton's on my list, too. May not be time for any pictures."

"I'll be happy to wait until it's convenient," Leo said. "My associate and I have come a long way for this opportunity. We can wait until your business with these cowboys is finished. And I'd be glad to take a look at your brother's arm."

Earp nodded, but it was Jacques who spoke.

"Or we can help you get rid of the men who, as you say, are out to get you."

Earp gave Jacques a look that could have been disdain. "I appreciate the offer, Mr. LeDieux, but these boys are gunmen who won't be easy to take down."

Jacques shrugged, giving Earp a thin smile. "Leo and I have seen our share of so-called bad men . . . first in New Orleans, and in many other places since. Killing a man is easy, so long as you know what you are doing."

Earp looked Jacques over again, his eyes making a closer inspection of the Cajun sailor. "You don't look like the type, Mr. LeDieux. These are professional gunmen."

Jacques's smile faded. "I own several guns, Marshal Earp, and I assure you I know how to use them. It was only an offer of assistance . . . only if you need it."

Holliday and Earp looked to Leo for an explanation, as if they both doubted Jacques's ability to be of any help with the problem Earp faced.

"Let me assure you, gentlemen," Leo said, "Jacques is as good at killing a man as anyone I've ever known. If the time comes, and you need our help, we'll be only too happy to oblige you. While this isn't our fight, we wouldn't ignore a request to bring the odds into balance."

Holliday nudged Earp with an elbow. "Don't turn down any offer, Wyatt," he said. "With Morgan and Virgil out of it, you may need all the help you can get."

"Speaking of help, Marshal," Leo said, "on the way up here from Tucson, we ran into a party of settlers who'd been ambushed by Indians. The driver of our wagon, a man named Barnes, said it looked like the work of Geronimo, who is reported to have escaped from the San Carlos reservation."

Earp glanced at Holliday, his eyes worried.

"There were several young people and some women who were slaughtered along with the men," Jacques added.

"Geronimo's a bad hombre, all right," Earp said. "I don't think he's dumb enough to give us any trouble here in Tombstone, but he may attack some of the miners up in the San Pedro's if he's not corralled soon."

Earp touched his hat brim. He spoke to Leo. "I'll send a wire to the army about those settlers, Doc LeMat. If Geronimo has escaped from San Carlos again like you say, they'll want to know the direction he took. There's not much else I can do, besides send out a burial party an' notify the commander at Fort Grant."

"I understand," Leo said as Holliday turned away from the door.

"Thanks again, Leo," Holliday said. "Maybe I'm gonna live after all . . . at least long enough to win another poker game and bed another whore."

"I'll let you know tomorrow about that picture," Earp said before he left the doorway. "Like I said, I may have my hands full with the rest of those cowboys. You came at a real bad time. I'll get word to you tomorrow mornin', around ten o'clock, after I make arrangements to get my brothers out of town."

"I understand," Leo said. "I'm willing to wait,

or as my associate suggested, we'd be willing to help with your . . . problem here." He turned his attention to Holliday. "After I visit the local apothecary, I'll have compounds for the infection in your hip, and perhaps a tonic that will ease your coughing spells with the tuberculosis. Come by my room tomorrow and we'll see if the apothecary has what I need."

"Hell, Leo," Holliday said. "I'm dying anyway, maybe a bit faster now. But I'd appreciate anything you can do to stop this damn pain in my ass. Wyatt has always been a pain in the ass, but this is worse. I can hardly sit down at a poker table in the shape I'm in. I'd just as soon be dead as too crippled to play a game of poker."

Leo grinned, although after examining Holliday's wound and witnessing the advanced stage of his tuberculosis, he knew the man must be withstanding a tremendous amount of suffering. "As far as I know, there's no treatment for your lung disease, Dr. Holliday. However I feel certain I can provide you with relief for your hip wound."

Earp seemed anxious to leave. "We'll talk tomorrow, Doc LeMat. I'm gonna have to give this picture-paintin' idea a bit more thought. Until things quiet down around Tombstone, I may not have the time."

"As I said, Marshal," Leo remarked, "my associate and I may be able to help. Just let us know if our help is needed."

Earp gave Leo another fleeting look. "I imagine this is the sort of thing I'll have to take care of myself . . . unless you're as good with that shoulder gun as Doc thinks you are."

Later that afternoon, Jacques and Leo discussed the conversation they'd had with Earp.

"It would appear that Marshal Earp does not think we are up to helping him with his problems with these so-called cowboys," Leo said.

Jacques grinned, his hand unconsciously moving to the handle of the knife in his scabbard. "Perhaps it is our fine clothing that has mislead the marshal into thinking we are gentlemen and not tough enough to face these Wild West desperadoes."

"Maybe the marshal should take the advice I gave Henry Stanley and look into your eyes, my friend," Leo said with a smile. "Then he would have no misconceptions about your toughness, as you call it."

Jacques smiled grimly. "What were the names Monsieur Earp mentioned that were still bothering him?"

Leo thought for a moment before answering. "I believe it was Ike Clanton, Ringo, and a man with the improbable name of Curly Bill."

Jacques nodded and got his battered hat off a

hat rack in the corner of the room. He walked to the door. "I believe I will take a walk around town, visit some of the local watering holes, as these westerners call them, and see for myself who these characters are . . . Curly and Ike and Ringo. I'll find you later.

Chapter 10

Ike Clanton was seething, tossing back drinks at the Red Dog Saloon less than two blocks away from the O.K. Corral, where his younger brother had died. Curly Bill Brocius sat across a plank table from Ike in the tented drinking parlor which led out back to an opium den known as the China Tiger. Curly Bill had been puffing on a water pipe since the middle of the afternoon and it showed.

"We gotta find a way," Ike said, his words slurred by half a quart of cheap whiskey flavored with ginger.

The pupils of Curly Bill's eyes were dilated and glassy, and his face was slack. "There's one real good way, Ike. We ambush the son of a bitch someplace. Pick a spot he walks at night an' we'll blow the bastard to hell. We'll try to find a way to take Doc Holliday down with him, the son of a bitch. He'll die just like any ordinary man if we catch him just right—up close, so there won't be no way he can survive it. Same goes for them other Earp brothers."

"I hear Morgan can't use his arm," Ike said. "If that's the truth, he won't be able to help Wyatt." Ike happened to see a short fellow wearing a sailor's cap sitting at the table beside them. The stranger to Tombstone appeared to be paying no attention to what they said, sipping on a shot of whiskey.

"Yeah. An' Virgil's got a bad leg, so he ain't out for no walks at night, either," Curly Bill remembered.

"What about Doc?" Ike asked.

"He's been hobblin' around on a cane. Got shot in the hip. Some say it was your little brother who got him."

"Poor Billy," Ike sighed. "My ma ain't quit cryin' since we buried him."

"It's time to put Wyatt Earp under for what he done to you and the McLaurys."

Ike studied the canvas flap leading out onto Fremont Street, a road now blanketed by darkness. "Where's Ringo?" he asked, downing another shot of rotgut.

"With that cut-up whore. He's been dead drunk for three solid days, shacked up with that bitch an' a gallon of Meskin tequila."

"What cut-up whore?"

"Molly . . . the one who got her ears nearly cut off by that drunk gambler last year."

Ike tilted his head. "I ain't real sure I could screw a woman who ain't got no ears. Ears can be a mighty important part of a woman sometimes."

"She wears her hair down over 'em so it's hard to tell, 'specially in the dark," Curly Bill said. "She's got big tits, an' that's damn near all Ringo cares about. Ears is just ears, if a man ain't gonna look at 'em close."

Ike frowned, remembering something. "A shoeshine boy told me this pistoleer came to town today in a fancy black buggy. He met up with Doc Holliday this afternoon, the boy said. He also told me this gent carries a gun under his coat. He knocked some wagon driver on his ass north of town an' pulled his gun on him, swearin' he was gonna kill him if'n he whipped his mules again. Didn't make a helluva lot of sense to me. Who the hell would kill a man over a team of goddamn mules, unless they was stolen or somethin'."

"It don't matter if he is a friend of Doc's," Curly Bill said, tipping back a shot of tequila. "We'll just shoot the dandy cur if he gets in the way."

"We gotta find a way to kill Wyatt," Ike said, tears brimming in his eyes. "He's gonna pay for helpin' to kill my little brother. I swear it! Doc Holliday's gonna get what's coming to him, too."

"Go talk to Ringo," Curly Bill said. "I'll go with you an' we'll lay it all out. There'll be others who'll help us. We got plenty of friends in

Cochise County. Them Earp boys showed up an' tried to take over the whole damn town."

"All that matters is havin' Wyatt Earp layin' in a grave next to Billy's," Ike whispered thickly. "I'm gonna drop my pants an' shit right in front of his headstone after we get it done."

"He don't deserve no better," Curly Bill said, waving for the bartender to bring him another shot of tequila. "While you're just sittin' here I'm gonna go out back to the Tiger an' have another plug of that crazy smoke."

"You hadn't oughta do business with them Chinks, Bill," Ike said. "They're liable to poison you with that shit one of these days."

"It makes me feel good," Curly Bill replied as his fresh drink arrived. "Hell, when I'm smokin' that crazy smoke I feel ten feet tall. Ain't scared of nothin'."

Ike was still staring out the tent flap. The dark street was full of traffic, mostly miners on their way to saloons or whorehouses in this part of town. "After you get back we'll go find Ringo an' that whore without no ears. If he'll back us, then it don't matter about Doc Holliday or nobody else."

"Earp's as good as dead right now. Hell, you know there ain't nobody quicker with a pistol than Johnny Ringo when it comes to a fight."

"I just wish he'd been there a few weeks ago,"

Ike said. "Things would have turned out different if you an' him had been sidin' with us."

"Ringo was with that whore over on Allen Street, in the cribs. He didn't know you was gonna fight the Earps until it was all over with. Besides, I hear tell you ran off soon as the shootin' started . . . that you hid behind the store soon as Billy went down."

"I didn't have no gun. Earp an' his bunch come after us before we was ready. Hell, it wasn't even noon yet. As to Ringo, I reckon he was drunk or he'd have showed up to help us with 'em."

"Hell, yes, he was drunk. I was with him the night before at the Tiger an' he'd been puffin' on crazy smoke half the night. I woulda been there myself if I hadn't been drunk the next mornin'. Nobody told me you boys was gonna take on the Earps an' Holliday so damn early. You shoulda waited until me an' Ringo got sober, so's we coulda helped."

"We'll go talk to Ringo," Ike said a moment later. "He told me he hates Doc with a passion, an' he ain't got no use for Wyatt neither."

"We been talkin' about this for weeks," Curly Bill said as he finished off his tequila. "Time we quit talkin' about it and got it done."

"Yeah," Ike said softly, hooding his eyelids. "The time for talkin' is over with. You go have that smoke, an' then we'll go talk to Ringo. Billy Claiborne will throw in with us, an' you know there'll be others after we get the word out. Us cowboys have gotta stick together."

Curly Bill stood up, a bit unsteady on his feet after all the opium and alcohol. "We'll just gun the bastards down some night real soon when they ain't expectin' us. It'll be easy. Morgan's the one who killed your little brother. We'll kill that sumbitch too, bad arm an' all."

"What about Sheriff Behan?" Ike asked.

"He don't like them Earps no better than we do. He won't lift a finger to stop us. If he does, we'll put him down same as the others."

Curly Bill sauntered out a back flap of the tent, turning down an alley for the China Tiger. Ike sat there a moment, toying with his glass, thinking about revenge.

Ringo watched Molly brush her long brown hair over the missing tips of her ears. He was lying on her bed in his undershorts, still nursing the remnants of a gallon jug of tequila.

Molly saw him watching her in the mirror. "How come you're starin' at me, Johnny."

"I was lookin' at your goddamn ears. You hadn't oughta tried to rob him."

"He was drunk," Molly said, a flush coming to her cheeks. "He beat the hell outta me, so I figured I had some extra money comin'."

Ringo chuckled, his steely eyes locked on the reflection of her face. "Cost you a couple of ears, you stupid bitch. There ain't enough money in the whole damn world to buy a new pair."

Tears sparkled in the corners of Molly's eyes. "How come you're bein' so mean to me, Johnny?"

"'Cause I never did like a woman without the right amount of ears, that's why."

"But you told me you loved me last night."

"Hell, that was just drunk talk. Who the hell's gonna love a whore with pieces of her ears cut off?"

"You can be cold as hell sometimes."

"I'm just tellin' you the truth. A woman's face don't look right with the tops of her ears missin'."

Ringo stiffened when he heard footsteps outside Molly's door. "Who the hell is that gonna be?" he whispered, reaching for the gun belt hanging on a bedpost.

"How should I know?" Molly replied, just as a soft knock sounded on her door.

"Get back out of the way," Ringo snarled, coming off the bed with his Colt .44 drawn. "I'll kill the sumbitch an' we won't have no more interruptions."

"Don't shoot nobody here, please!"

"Shut up an' get over there in the corner." Ringo eased to the door, his gun ready. "Who is it?" he asked softly, standing to one side of the doorjamb in case bullets came flying through the thin planking.

"It's me, Ike," a clogged voice said. "Curly Bill is with me."

Ringo lowered his pistol and reached for the door latch. "How the hell'd you know where to find me?" he asked, opening the door a crack.

Curly Bill was leering drunkenly. "I told Ike where you was, Johnny. We got business to talk over."

He allowed them to enter Molly's small, stuffy room as Molly pulled her corset strings together over her melon-size breasts.

"I ain't in the mood to talk business," Ringo replied, his expression sour. "Hell, I'm still tryin' to get drunk enough to mount this bitch."

Ike and Curly Bill nodded to Molly. "It's real important, Ringo," Ike said. "We got us a plan to get rid of Wyatt Earp an' his brothers for good . . . an' that includes that lunger, ol' Doc Holliday."

"I'm gonna get Holliday myself one of these days for what he done to me at the Oriental that night. He tried to make a damn fool outta me."

"We need to go someplace an' talk," Curly Bill said after a glance at Molly. "Meet us over at the Tiger in 'bout half an hour."

"I ain't done with this whore yet," Ringo protested.

Curly Bill grinned. "You can come back an' finish up your business soon as we're done talkin'. Get dressed an' come on up the back alley behind

Allen Street to the Tiger. You're gonna like what we's aimin' to do."

Ringo gave Molly a scowl. "You run fetch me some more of this tequila while I'm gone," he said.

"But I ain't got no money, Johnny," she said.

Ringo walked over to his denims, which were draped across the back of a bullhide chair. "Here's eight dollars. See if there's enough left over so you can buy yourself some new ears."

All three men laughed. Molly lowered her eyes to the dirt floor and said nothing.

"I'll see you boys in half an hour at the Tiger," Ringo said.

"We'll be waitin'," Ike told him as they started out of the room.

A pale moon illuminated the street when Ike spotted a short man who looked out of place watching them walk up the alley to the China Tiger. The man was wearing a sailor's cap. All manner of tattoos covered his forearms where they showed below his bulging shirtsleeves. He looked vaguely familiar.

"What's that little swabbie starin' at?" Ike asked, pausing in the alley.

Curly Bill gave the stranger a passing glance. "Who gives a shit, Ike? He ain't gonna give us no trouble. Hell, we're cowboys, an' he ain't even carryin' a gun. You worry too goddamn much."

Ike started up the alley again. "It always did bother me when some son of a bitch stared at me."

Curly Bill stopped again near the back entrance into the Tiger. "You want me to go back an' shoot the little bastard just for starin' at you?"

"Naw. We don't need no more trouble until we get ready to make our move against them Earps an' Holliday," Ike replied, pushing the tent flap out of the way to enter the smoky den filled with the sweet scent of opium.

"Bring us a pipe, you little yellow bastard," Curly Bill said to a slender Asian wearing a silky robe. "An' make it damn quick."

The man bowed and hurried off to an adjoining tent while Ike and Curly Bill found places on soft rugs in the darkness of the tent.

"We're gonna kill that bastard Earp," Ike said. "Same goes for Holliday."

"Won't be nothin' to it, if we do it my way," Curly Bill said. "We ambush the bastards one night real soon. Won't nobody even know who done it. . . ."

After he left, they lit the pipes, inhaled deeply, and lay back against soft pillows arranged on the rugs. As the opium took effect, their eyes became glassy and unfocused, dreams of revenge swirling in their addled brains.

After a few minutes, Curly Bill glanced languidly at Ike. "You keepin' track of the time?" he asked in a slurred, sleepy voice.

Ike looked back at him with a blank face. "Hell no. Why?"

Curly Bill raised himself up on one elbow. "'Cause it wouldn't do to keep Ringo waitin'," he said, taking another drag on the pipe. "We're supposed to meet him here later. He won't like it if'n we're too messed up to talk about our plans."

Ike shrugged. "Hell with Ringo. He should've been there at the O.K. Corral. Things would've been different if he'd been there."

Curly Bill lowered the pipe. "Why don't you tell him that, Ike? I'd sure like to see his reaction if you insinuate he's yellow. "

Ike's eyes showed fear. "That ain't what I said, Curly Bill."

"Yeah, well if'n I was you, I'd be real careful what you say to Ringo. He's mean as a snake an' has a real hair trigger."

Ike nodded, staring at the smoke drifting up from his pipe.

Chapter 11

Leo was enjoying brisket of beef *a la flambé* in champagne sauce at the Cosmopolitan Hotel's Maison Doree when Jacques came into the café. For a so-called frontier town, Tombstone's Maison Doree was excellent and he'd been enjoying himself, even though he ate alone. The restaurant, despite its exquisite food, was only half full. Leo supposed it was the time of year, with the nearness of winter keeping travelers off the roads westward to California, where snows and bad weather might catch them in the mountains—or worse, in the desert flats farther to the south where draft animals might perish without water.

The furnishings in the Maison Doree were as elegant as most of the finer restaurants in New Orleans or San Antonio, including the stately St. Anthony Hotel Café on the ground floor beneath Leo's suite of rooms. Etched mirrors lined the walls of the Maison Doree, and the tables and rugs were expensive, befitting one of the better eating establishments anywhere. Crystal chandeliers hung from the ceiling, casting sparkling light over the tables and polished mahogany furniture. Spotless linen tablecloths covered every table.

Jacques took a seat across from Leo, removing his seaman's cap. "I found the men Marshal Earp and Dr. Holliday seem so worried about," he said without bothering to explain where he'd been or why he'd been so long.

"Ike Clanton? And Curly Bill Brocius?" Leo asked, dipping his steak in the creamy white sauce.

"*Oui, mon ami*, and the one called Johnny Ringo."

"Tell me about them."

A waitress appeared to take Jacques's order. She gave him a dark look when she noticed his manner of dress, for most of the patrons wore proper evening attire. "A glass of red wine, and a choice piece of brisket in champagne sauce like the one my friend is having."

"Potatoes?" she asked.

"Fried. Is there anything else west of the Mississippi?"

"We can bake them," she offered curtly, taking a closer look at Jacques and his rather slovenly dress, as though his appearance, and the question, offended her.

"Fry them," Jacques said impatiently, waving her away with the back of his hand.

"You're out of sorts, old friend. What is it that brings on your foul mood?"

"This town," Jacques replied. "It is a shithole, a city of tents and men of low breeding."

Leo stifled a chuckle. "Are you now an authority on the breeding of men, Monsieur LeDieux? Do you lay claim to a blue-blooded ancestry yourself?"

Jacques ignored the question. "Ike Clanton is a common saddletramp. He frequents a tent saloon known as the Red Dog, a gathering place for men who dislike the use of bathwater on a regular basis, or so it would seem. The place had a terrible smell."

Leo was enjoying himself, and his meal. "You made this judgment based solely on Mr. Clanton's scent? Or were his hands also dirty?"

Jacques's flinty eyes darkened. "He is an unwashed cowboy of the lowest type. And his friend, Curly Bill Brocius, is no better. They spent a great deal of time in an opium den behind the saloon."

Leo nodded. "I take it that Chinese merchants have discovered Tombstone."

"It's called the China Tiger. A tent, like most of the places here. They provide water pipes where anyone can buy plugs of blue opium gum."

"Clanton and Brocius, do they carry guns?"

Jacques wagged his head. "Not Clanton. He wears no gun or holster. Brocius, on the other hand, has two pistols tied low on his leg in the fashion of a gunfighter."

"You'd judge him to be dangerous?"

"No. He's a coward . . . I can see it in his eyes. He is a braggart, but he has no backbone. In my opinion, neither does Ike Clanton."

"You got close to them? To Clanton and Brocius?"

"I sat beside them at a table at the Red Dog, and then I followed them to a whore's crib where they talked to Johnny Ringo. I overheard what they plan to do."

"What's Ringo like?"

Jacques frowned as his glass of wine arrived. He waited until the waitress left their table. "Ringo will be the deadly one. I only saw him for a moment, as Clanton and Brocius were leaving the whore's room, but he has the eyes of a cat. Ringo misses nothing."

Leo was suddenly serious, laying his fork beside his plate. "You rarely ever say these things about another man, Jacques. I know how well you read others."

"He will be a difficult adversary, *mon ami*. He will be a hard man to kill, if it becomes necessary to kill him for the sake of becoming a closer associate of Marshal Earp's."

"He's one of the men Marshal Earp and Dr. Holliday feel are their enemies in the continuation of this conflict at the corral on Fremont."

Jacques tasted his drink. "Ringo will be the one to watch. I think Clanton is mostly talk. Brocius may only be brave when he is drunk, or smoking opium. Ringo, on the other hand, will be dangerous under any circumstances." Jacques paused, "And the other men all seem to have a great respect for his quickness with a handgun."

"I need to get a look at him myself," Leo said. "While we came to Tombstone to paint Marshal Earp's portrait, we may find ourselves involved in his difficulties. I want to get a look at all three of them . . . Ike Clanton, Curly Bill, and most of all, Johnny Ringo, since you say he's the most dangerous one of the three."

"Without a doubt, Leo," Jacques said, casting a glance around the ornately decorated dining room. "Ringo is a man I would never turn my back on. Better to kill him early than to worry about having him behind you."

"We can't simply kill a man over the way he looks," Leo said.

Jacques gave him a curious glance. "And why not? It would be a simple matter to slip into the whore's crib tonight to cut his throat. No one would ever know, and then you could make the arrangements with Marshal Earp to have him sit for his portrait."

Leo resumed eating, for his brisket was growing cold. "You disappoint me, Jacques. I've done everything within my power to make a civilized man of you, despite your clouded upbringing. I find I've wasted my time. Your solution to our dilemma is to commit outright murder in the name of artistry. In my view, there would be blood on my canvas." He chuckled softly after he said it.

Jacques glanced up from his wineglass. "And would this be the first canvas you painted without any bloodstains, *mon ami*?"

Leo chewed thoughtfully a moment. "Those days are behind me, Jacques. From now on I intend to live quietly as a portraitist. Let's change the subject."

Jacques saw his brisket being carried toward him on a tray by their plump waitress. "I have a feeling, Leo, that before the paint can dry on this canvas you intend to finish, there will be blood on your hands. I know you too well to believe otherwise."

Leo sorted through his thoughts while Jacques cut into his piece of beef. "Dr. John Holliday is the one who fascinates me the most," he said. "He may also be worthy of a portrait. He has no obvious signs of a killer about him, yet there is something there . . . I find it hard to define."

"His wound is serious?" Jacques asked around a mouthful of brisket.

"No. Infection has set in. I can cure that. But I'm afraid his lung disease is fatal. It's only a matter of time before he succumbs to it."

"I've heard it called the 'galloping consumption,'" Jacques said. "People all over New Orleans died from it, like the Yellow Fever epidemic years ago."

"A dry climate such as this is the best remedy, although it only slows down the progression of the disease."

"He's in the right place," Jacques observed. "This is by far the driest place we've ever been. If dust and heat are a remedy for tuberculosis, Dr. Holliday has found the perfect spot to live."

"You complain about everything," Leo said. "This is some of the best beef we've had in months."

Jacques looked around for their waitress. "Perhaps so, Leo, but it goes down better with a glass of water and more wine. My throat is like sand."

Leo considered what Jacques had told him. Ike Clanton was not the gunman to be feared. Curly Bill Brocius could be dangerous with his brain addled by opium, and he wore his guns in the fashion of a shootist.

But if Johnny Ringo made such a deep impression on Jacques, there was reason for concern. Jacques knew hardened men like some liverymen knew the dispositions of horses.

Leo made up his mind to see all three men for himself.

* * *

They were eating lemon pie when the first angry voice rang out.

"You're a dead son of a bitch, Virgil!"

"What was that?" a woman at a nearby table asked, putting down her fork.

The gentleman dining with her raised his hand to his lips for silence. "That's Billy Claiborne. Be quiet, darling, for it is none of our affair."

Leo opened the left lapel of his coat. Jacques pushed his plate of pie aside.

"Leave it alone, Billy!" another voice shouted. "It's over between us."

"Like hell! You an' your goddamn brothers killed Frank an' his brother."

"Go home, Billy!"

"It ain't over 'til the last of you damn Earps is dead. I reckon you know it's just started between us."

"Go on home, Billy."

"You can't just up an' shoot three cowboys in Tombstone like you done. There's a debt to be paid."

Leo arose from his chair. Jacques got up and followed him to the front door.

Two men were facing each other in the street— a man on crutches, and a lanky cowboy with a gun tied low on his leg. People on the boardwalks were cautiously backing away.

"We's gonna kill you an' your goddamn brothers, Virgil. You an' your bastard kin are gonna be on Boot Hill afore this is over."

Leo opened the door and walked out on the front porch of the Cosmopolitan. Jacques was a few feet behind him, off to his right.

The man on crutches had no gun Leo could see, and it seemed a one-sided affair. During a moment of quiet between the two men, Leo spoke to the man wearing the gun. "Leave it alone, my friend," Leo said. "The man you've challenged is obviously not able to defend himself tonight."

"Mind your own goddamn business," the gunman snarled, his face turned briefly toward Leo.

"I am minding my own business," Leo replied, his voice calm, steady. "I was having a quiet dinner when your shouts interrupted my meal. Loud noises are hard on my digestion and I urge you to reconsider."

"Who the hell are you, an' what's your stake in this?" the gunman demanded.

"My name's of little importance. I am Leo LeMat, and my stake in this, as you put it, is to allow my brisket to digest properly."

"Do you know who I am? Are you crazy, mister?"

"Not to any extent that I'm aware of," Leo answered, tired of the talk, reaching into his coat for his pistol. He took it out, cocked it, and aimed it into the street with his sights set on the gunman's chest. "As to knowing who you are, I couldn't care less. The undertaker may need your name. All I want from you is silence. Unless you wish to fill a pine box tonight, turn around and go back wherever you came from at once. Otherwise, you have my solemn word that I'll kill you if you continue."

A crowd had begun to gather along the boardwalks. Someone said, "His name's Billy Claiborne, mister."

"Ah," Leo sighed. "As I recall, you were one of the men who ran off and hid during that shooting at the O.K. Corral last month. It would seem you're short on nerve unless the man you're facing is unarmed."

Claiborne stared into the barrel of Leo's gun, then he took a deep breath and relaxed the hand near his gun. "What did you say your name was, mister?" he asked.

"Leo LeMat. I'm staying here at the Cosmopolitan Hotel."

"I'll tell some of the other cowboys about you . . . about how you interfered."

"Have it printed in the newspaper for all I care," Leo replied. "Just make damn sure you don't interrupt my dinner again. It seems a small thing, a poor reason to kill a man."

Claiborne backed away, then he took off down Allen Street with his fists balled.

The man on crutches hobbled over to Leo. "Thanks for what you did. I'm Virgil Earp, an' in case you didn't know it, this town is fixin' to have another string of killings . . . unless somebody can stop it."

Leo took Virgil Earp's handshake. "A pleasure to meet you, Mr. Earp. I met your brother Wyatt earlier today. I came to Tombstone to paint his portrait."

"His what?"

LeMat sighed. "His picture. You see, I'm a painter by profession. . . ."

Virgil's eyebrows raised. "For a painter, you took quite a chance bracing Billy down."

Leo wagged his head. "Not as much as you might think, Mr. Earp. For you see, Billy Claiborne is a coward. It is evident in his eyes."

Virgil smiled and nodded. "Coward or no, a man with a gun can still kill you."

"Not if his hand is as slow as his mind," Leo said, turning and going back to his pie.

Chapter 12

.

Ike saw Billy Claiborne rush through the tent flap into the Red Dog. "Yonder's Billy," he said to Curly Bill and Ringo. "I wonder how come he's in such a hurry?"

Billy saw them seated at a table near the back and came over at a brisk walk. "Trouble," Billy said without explaining what he meant. He was lean to the point of being skinny, and his red hair set him apart from most of the other patrons. He took pride in the way he waxed his handlebar mustache, curling it up at the ends.

"What sorta trouble?" Curly Bill asked, weaving in his chair from the several plugs of opium he had smoked at the China Tiger since the middle of the afternoon.

Billy glanced around him to see who might be listening. "I called out Virgil Earp a while ago. Caught him walkin' down the street in front of the Cosmopolitan Hotel, on crutches, by hisself. I sure as hell meant to kill him, only this stranger got into it."

"That wasn't smart," Ringo said. "Too many witnesses, Billy. You can't jump one of Wyatt's brothers right in the middle of the business district. You shoulda had better sense than to do that."

Ike tried to read Billy's face. Billy's hands were still shaking from his encounter with Virgil Earp, and that made Ike wonder.

"It was a witness who kept me from killin' him," Billy went on.

"A witness?" Ike asked.

"Some tall son of a bitch in a black coat. He come out of the hotel an' drew down on me before I could kill Virgil. He even told me his name." Billy hooked his thumbs in his gunbelt to keep his hands from trembling and looked around for a waiter to bring him some whiskey to calm his nerves. When he saw the man waiting on a nearby table, he called out, "Whiskey, an' be quick about it."

"What was his name?" Ringo asked before Ike could frame the same question.

"LeMat. Leo LeMat. A crazy bastard. He said that I was keepin' him from the right kind of digestion for his goddamn dinner an' that he'd kill me if I didn't clear out. Can you imagine that? A son of a bitch worried about indigestion steppin' into a damn gunfight, all on account of his belly?"

Curly Bill chuckled. "He was worried about a bellyache?"

"Real worried. He stuck his pistol right in my face," Billy said.

"It's that friend of Doc's," Ike offered. "He's the same bastard who jerked a gun on that mule skinner this afternoon. You say his name is LeMat? Sounds like the same feller, by the way you tell it."

"Leo LeMat. That's what he said." Billy sounded very sure of it.

The waiter appeared and placed a tumbler of amber-colored liquid in front of him. Billy grabbed the glass and upended it, spilling some on his chin as he drank it down in one convulsive swallow.

"Never heard of him," Curly Bill mumbled, reaching for his glass of tequila. "How come you didn't just kill the sumbitch an' be done with it?"

"'Cause he had the drop on me—that's why. He had his gun hid inside his coat. I wasn't expectin' him to come out with no pistol."

"He's the same one," Ike said again. "He took up with Virgil an' Doc Holliday, an' that's proof of where he lies. Maybe Wyatt even brought him to town to help 'em, on account of Virgil an' Morgan bein' hurt, an' Doc Holliday with a bullet in his ass, so's they can't go up against us on the square. We all know that Wyatt don't fight fair."

Billy's eyes swept the table. "Let's go kill him. He said he was stayin' at the Cosmopolitan."

"He told you where he was stayin'?" Curly Bill said, as if he couldn't believe it.

"He damn sure did. He's either plumb loco, or he's new to these parts an' don't know about the cowboys . . . how we control things."

Ringo leaned back in his seat. "Maybe he ain't afraid of you, Billy. You didn't scare him none, seems like. If he was scared, he wouldn't have pulled no gun on you tonight when you was about to kill Virgil, like you say you was."

"I done told you he had the drop on me. Wasn't nothin' I could do. I say we all go over there an' kill the son of a bitch right now."

"That wouldn't be smart," Ringo replied. "It would draw too much attention to us. We'll find the right place and the right time to take him down, along with the Earps, whoever this Leo LeMat happens to be."

"It was plumb embarrassin'," Billy complained. "There was a whole bunch of folks who saw it happen. It ain't gonna look good for us cowboys."

"We're already figurin' on how we're gonna kill Wyatt," Ike said, keeping his voice low. "Pull up a chair and listen to what Johnny has to say."

"You mean you ain't gonna go back an' help me kill this LeMat feller?" Billy asked.

"Not now!" Ike told him harshly. "Just sit down

and shut the fuck up while Ringo tells us his plan for them Earps. We gotta do this smart, so we don't get blown all to hell like they done to us the last time."

"We gotta be ready," Curly Bill muttered, his head lolling to one side, his eyes shuttered by opium and liquor.

"Fetch a chair," Ike said. "This time, we're gonna be ready for 'em. Won't be no mistakes like there was the last time. We aim to make sure of it. Get a chair an' sit down an' shut up so we can hear what Ringo has to say."

Billy took an empty chair from a nearby table, paying only scant notice to a man wearing some sort of strange white cap as he came through the rear tent flap and walked over to the bar.

After listening to Ringo, Billy Claiborne spoke. "Here's another thing we can do. Geronimo broke from San Carlos again, along with a bunch of Apache warriors. They killed an' scalped this settler family north of Tombstone. The army from up at Fort Grant is lookin' for 'em, only they can't find their asses with both hands. Somebody reported it to Sheriff Behan. They sent out a burial party late this evenin'."

"What the hell has that got to do with killin' Wyatt an' Doc?" Curly Bill asked, his words slurred, his eyes focused as he held on to the edge of the table.

Billy lowered his voice even more. "We make it look like Geronimo killed them Earps an' Holliday. We shoot 'em, an' then we scalp 'em. Everybody'll blame Geronimo an' his Apaches for it an' we get off clean."

"You ever scalped a man, Billy?" Ringo asked.

"No," he said after a moment of thought, "but I seen plenty of it in my time. There ain't nothin' to it. All you do is cut off the sumbitch's hair."

"There's more to it," Ringo said, pouring tequila into a smudged glass. "You've gotta know where to cut if off so it'll look like an Apache done it."

"What goddamn difference does it make?" Billy asked, staring at Ringo. "Who the hell's gonna look that close? Folks around here are gonna be ready to blame Geronimo an' his red savages for nearly anything."

"I ain't so sure," Ike said.

"Me neither," Curly Bill added. "Besides, who wants to go to all that trouble, givin' them boys a haircut?"

Ringo turned his attention to the bar where a man seemed to be listening to them, but when he saw the little gent's strange clothing and nondescript cap, he returned to the conversation at the table. "We want folks to know it was the cowboys who got even with the Earps an' Doc Holliday. It's a waste of time if we try an' make people think Injuns did it. The cowboys run this county.

We don't take shit off nobody and we need to make a point that if anybody crosses us they're bound for boot hill in a hurry."

"Amen to that," Curly Bill said. "We gotta teach some of these uppity bastards a lesson about who runs things around here."

Ike nodded. "It'll remind 'em of what happened when them goddamn Earps come after my brother an' the McLaurys. We can't let that go unpunished."

"I agree with Ike," Curly Bill muttered, his chin almost resting on his chest. "Let's just kill the bastards from ambush an' be done with it."

A silence followed. Drinkers in the Red Dog Saloon continued with their noisy conversations about silver dust and whores.

"We need to find the right place," Ringo said. "Maybe catch at least two of the Earps together some night. Doc Holliday will be with his whore, or at the Oriental, so he'll be easy to cut down when it closes. We split up into pairs. Each of us will have a target."

"I like the idea," Ike said.

"But what about that bastard stayin' at the Cosmopolitan?" Billy wanted to know. "What are we gonna do about him?"

"One of us will take care of him," Ringo replied. "Holliday is the shootist, even when he's drunk, so I'm gonna take him personally an' make damn sure he's dead. One of you can take this LeMat when he comes out of the hotel. Just shoot the bastard in the back."

"I'll take him," Billy said. "After what he done to me in front of all those folks, I'm gonna enjoy killin' him, even if I do gun him from behind."

"All that matters is that we get rid of 'em," Ike said. "I can see who else will side with us. Them Baxter boys ain't got no love for Wyatt, after he run 'em out of the Oriental back in the spring, claimin' they was cheatin' at monte."

"It won't take many of us," Ringo said, "if we each do the jobs we set out to do."

"When do we go after 'em?" Ike asked.

"Real soon," Ringo told him. "Everybody find out who's willin' to help us . . . men we can trust, men who know how to use a gun." He glanced down at Ike's waist. "And everybody remember to bring a goddamn gun."

Jacques slipped quietly out of the tent after paying his bar bill. He walked down Allen Street in almost total darkness, his mind filled with the things he'd overheard at the table near the back of the Red Dog.

"All this for a painting," he muttered, his hands shoved deep into his pants pockets.

His unwavering loyalty to Leo brought him closer to a decision—to take the dangerous man out of the fight that was sure to come.

He knew where Johnny Ringo stayed, in the soiled dove's crib only a block away.

"I can kill him easily," Jacques said to himself, though he knew Ringo would be a cautious man.

But Leo had forbidden it at suppertime, leaving Jacques with few choices. If a knife blade suddenly ended the life of Johnny Ringo, Leo would know who was responsible for the killing.

Jacques made for the Cosmopolitan Hotel, passing dozens of drunken miners along the way.

"If only Leo was not so stubborn," he whispered.

To Jacques, slitting the throat of a man like Ringo was little more than swatting a fly.

"There were four of them," Jacques said. "The one named Billy Claiborne came not long after we finished our dinner. He knew the others well. I overheard what he said to them."

"They plan to kill the Earps and Doc Holliday?" Leo asked, pouring himself a brandy in the lamplight inside his room at the Cosmopolitan.

"*Oui*," he replied. "And they intend to kill you. I heard them talking."

"I've been an assassin's target before," Leo said, taking a sip of brandy. "Not to worry. Not yet, until we know how and when they mean to do it."

"They are planning some sort of ambush, and

soon," Jacques told him. "Johnny Ringo told the others to be sure to bring their guns."

"Soon?" Leo asked, sarcasm tinging his deep voice. "I'd hoped to enjoy the sights a bit longer."

"Do not take it so lightly, *mon ami*," Jacques said, an eye to one open window. "This Ringo is no fool. As I told you before, he will be a hard man to kill . . . if he is ready for it. With your permission, I'll go back to the whore's crib on Allen Street and silence him forever."

"Not yet," Leo said.

Jacques spread his palms. "But why should we wait?"

Leo took a deep breath. "This isn't our fight. We came here to paint Wyatt Earp's portrait. And after meeting John Holliday, I may ask him to sit for me as well. Nothing can get in the way of our reason for being here."

"But they are plotting to kill you, Leo, for no better reason than stopping Claiborne from killing Virgil Earp here tonight."

"Let them plot," Leo said, an icy tone changing his voice. "They won't be the first to believe a bullet could silence me. As of now, all the others have all been proven wrong."

Jacques said no more, leaving their hotel room even though the hour was late. He went downstairs, swinging toward the Red Dog with a plan of his own in mind. Leo had only said to leave Ringo and the others alive. He didn't say that a bit of persuasion couldn't be used to convince these so-called cowboys that making an attempt on Leo LeMat's life would be a big mistake.

As he walked, he pulled his knife from its scabbard and wiped the blade back and forth on his trousers, humming to himself in anticipation of his plans for the night.

Some men, like dogs that try to bite their masters, need to be taught manners. He intended to teach these cowboys that there are men with whom it is dangerous to interfere.

Chapter 13

After finishing off several bottles of whiskey and a couple more of tequila, Curly Bill, Ringo, Ike, and Billy Claiborne finalized their plans for the assassination of the Earp brothers and the troublesome stranger named LeMat.

"All right," Ringo said as he got to his feet. "We're clear on this then? We're gonna check with our friends an' see who's gonna stand with us against the Earps."

Curly Bill, Ike, and Billy all nodded, standing up from the table.

"Then we're gonna kill the bastards an' show this town who's the bosses," Ike said with satisfaction.

"What're you gonna do, Ringo?" Billy asked.

Ringo grinned. "I'm gonna go back to my woman. She's waitin, for me with a fresh bottle of tequila."

"How 'bout you, Curly Bill," Billy asked.

"Why are you askin', Billy?" Curly Bill asked. "You afraid to walk home in the dark alone?"

Ike grinned. "Yeah. You afraid that stranger might take another chance at you?"

Billy's face flushed red. "Hell, no. But the night's young yet, an' I thought we might go do some gamblin'."

Curly Bill shook his head. "Not me. I still got half a pipe left at the Tiger an' I intend to go finish it."

The men said their good-byes and left the saloon.

Jacques followed Curly Bill Brocius down the alley off of Allen Street, keeping to the deepest shadows. He'd been waiting for almost an hour outside the saloon. Curly Bill was weaving, staggering, aiming for the opium den named the China Tiger. The others, Johnny Ringo and Claiborne and several more, were still drinking at the Red Dog.

When Curly Bill made a turn for the China Tiger's tent, Jacques slipped up behind him with his dagger clenched in his fist.

"Stop, my friend," Jacques whispered, allowing Curly Bill to feel the tip of the blade against his spine as he grabbed the cowboy's shirt collar. "Take one more step and you will be a piece of carved meat."

Curly Bill glanced over his shoulder with liquor-fogged eyes.

"Who the hell are you?" he demanded.

"You might call me the angel of death . . . your death, if you do not listen to me very closely."

"You can kiss my ass," Curly Bill said. "You see this red sash around my waist? Means I'm a cowboy. Nobody talks to a cowboy like that in Tombstone."

Jacques jerked Curly Bill's collar and threw him down on his back in the alley. He jumped on the gunman's chest and put his dagger against Curly Bill's throat.

"To hell with cowboys and meaningless pieces of red cloth," Jacques hissed, jerking both of Curly Bill's pistols from their holsters. "I talk to you the way I talk to any piece of trash. I can kill you now and it will be quiet. No one will hear you scream with my hand over your mouth when I slit your throat. They will find you here in the morning, unless the stray dogs eat you first."

"Who the hell are you?" Curly Bill asked again as he felt the point of Jacques's knife prick his skin.

Jacques lowered his badly scarred face so Curly Bill could see him clearly. "A messenger."

"A messenger?"

Jacques nodded, putting a bit more pressure on his dagger so that now blood trickled from Curly Bill's neck. "I bring you a warning. I don't give a damn about the red sashes or cowboys or anything else in this shithole town. Make certain that you leave Dr. Leo LeMat alone, and the same goes for Wyatt Earp. You plan to kill Earp, you and your yellow-dog friends. I warn you against it, or you will die a horrible death. Your head will be lying in the street in front of Marshal Earp's office. Blackflies will be crawling in and out of your nose. The maggots will eat your brain and your flesh, but you will not feel any of this. You will be dead."

"Nobody can talk to a cowboy like that," Curly Bill said drunkenly, still defiant.

"But I am, *mon ami*, and I hope you take me seriously. If you, or any of your friends, come near Dr. LeMat or Wyatt Earp, you will pay for it with their lives."

"You're bluffin'." Curly Bill said. He swallowed hard, trying to see Jacques in the darkness of the alleyway.

"Then test me, you ignorant *batard*. I will show you just how serious I am."

"What the hell is a batard?"

Jacques had had enough conversation. There was a risk that someone would come down the alley at any moment. "I will leave you with a little something to remind you of my warning," he said savagely. "When you look in a mirror, it will remind you of the promise I have made."

With a suddenness Curly Bill did not expect, Jacques took his knife away from the gunman's throat and made a quick slashing motion across the tip of Curly Bill's left ear.

"You son of a—" Curly Bill shouted.

He did not finish what he intended to say. Jacques swung one of the gunman's pistols down, cracking the barrel over Curly Bill's head.

Curly Bill's body went slack and his eyelids drooped as blood slowly pumped from his ruined ear to stain the dirt around his head scarlet.

"Sleep well," Jacques whispered, standing up, tossing the gun aside.

As an afterthought, Jacques cut the red cloth around Curly Bill's waist. He tied it around the gunman's neck, chuckling softly over his joke When Curly Bill finally woke up he would be wearing a tightly knotted red bow tie.

He put his knife back in his boot and hurried away toward Allen Street, satisfied that Brocius and his friends would know how dangerous it could be to cross paths with Leo LeMat. Jacques had not violated his promise to Leo to let the gunmen plotting against Leo and Marshal Earp live . . . he had only given one of them a warning—one that the man would ignore at the peril of his life.

"Go for your gun, you cowardly sumbitch!"

Jacques heard the commotion as he was heading back to the hotel.

Two men were squared off in front of each other not far from the Red Dog Saloon.

"To hell with you!" the other cowboy cried.

Jacques had never seen either man before.

"You're sidin' with them goddamn Earps!" the first man bellowed. "That's enough to get you killed in this town."

"I'm just a friend of Virgil's. I'm not taking a side in any of this."

"Like hell! The cowboys run this town. Them Earp brothers can't just show up and take over Tombstone. If you're a friend of Virgil Earp's, you're an enemy of the cowboys, an' that makes you a marked man."

Jacques stepped wide of both men to be out of the line of fire. They each had hands poised near the butts of their pistols. The gunplay could start any minute. Though the street was dark, there was light enough for the gunmen to see each other. One man, the first to speak, was wearing a red sash around his waist similar to the one Curly Bill wore.

"A cowboy," Jacques whispered. It wasn't his fight, unless someone came after Leo, thus Jacques stepped up on a porch in front of a harness shop to watch what was going on. Men spilled out of the Red Dog and a couple of other drinking parlors to see what the ruckus was about.

Johnny Ringo emerged from the Red Dog. He immediately saw what was going on.

"Not now, Ned," Ringo said. "There'll be another time to settle this."

The cowboy named Ned glanced at Ringo, then back to the man facing him in the street. "I'm gonna kill him, Johnny. He's the one who told them Earp brothers an' Holliday that Ike and some of the boys was down at the O.K. Corral that day."

"I said to forget about it for now," Ringo said, a cold edge to his voice. "Go home. Don't start trouble tonight. You've had too damn much to drink."

Farther up the street, Jacques saw a figure limp out on the porch of the Oriental Saloon.

Doc Holliday, Jacques thought. He recognized him almost at once.

"Gentlemen!" Holliday cried, squaring himself. "Take your quarrel somewhere else. You disturb the peace and quiet of this city! How can I concentrate on a game of cards with all this shouting?"

"Stay out of this, Doc," Johnny Ringo said. "You've got a bullet in your ass and you're no match for me, so mind your own goddamn business."

"My, my," Holliday replied, grinning with no real humor in it. "Are you now calling yourself the local magistrate, Ringo? Is it your job to keep the peace? While I may have a bullet in my ass, as you say, I assure you I'm more than your equal. If you believe otherwise, then reach for your gun. We shall enjoy a contest of skills . . . yours against mine. Even though I have a bullet hole in one of my buttocks, it's a handicap I'll do my very best to overcome. May the best man win."

Ringo tensed.

Holliday laughed. "Having second thoughts, Mr. Ringo? All you have to do is draw. . . ."

The street became crowded with onlookers. Jacques wondered if he should take a side in this. Leo had talked about asking Holliday for the opportunity to paint his portrait after the one he intended to paint of Wyatt Earp. If Holliday was killed, Leo would be robbed of the opportunity.

"I'll get you, Doc," Ringo said.

Holliday's grin widened. "Pull your gun, you dog. You somehow missed all the fun at the O.K. Corral, but some men are lucky, they get second chances."

"I'm gonna kill you one of these days, Doc."

"Tonight could be your finest hour, Ringo. Try it now and no one will have to wait for the outcome. We can settle the minor disagreement between us this very evening, if you are so inclined."

Jacques saw a dark silhouette coming around behind the Red Dog Saloon, a man with a pistol in his fist. He recognized Billy Claiborne at once.

No matter what the outcome of the confrontation between Doc Holliday and Johnny Ringo might be, Jacques knew he had to take a hand in things now.

He stepped off the porch of the harness shop while everyone's attention was on Holliday and Ringo. No one, not even Billy Claiborne, noticed him as he crossed the road.

"Drop the gun," Jacques whispered, placing the barrel of his pistol against Claiborne's spine. "Do not turn around. Do not look at me. I will kill you if you disobey me. Let go of the gun."

"Holy shit," Billy stammered, stiffening when he felt cold iron touch his backbone.

"I said drop it."

Billy let the revolver fall. "Don't shoot me," he whimpered softly. "I was just seein' what all the yellin' was about."

"I know what you meant to do," Jacques said, picking up the fallen six-gun. "Stay here. If you move I promise you I will be the last thing you ever see."

"I won't," Billy swore. "I ain't gonna do nothin'. I swear it. "

"If you do," Jacques said, backing away, "your name will be in the obituary section of tomorrow's newspaper."

Jacques moved so silently Billy wasn't aware he was gone.

"Listen, mister . . . whoever you are," Billy continued, talking to emptiness. "I swear I wasn't gonna do nothin'."

Ringo, hearing Billy's voice, turned his back on Doc and walked over to him.

He looked behind Billy, and seeing no one stared at Billy's sweating, flushed face and the strange way Billy was holding his hands out from his sides.

"What the hell's goin' on, Billy?" Ringo asked, stepping in front of him.

"Ringo!" Billy said with relief. "I'm glad you're here. This son of a bitch is holdin' a gun on me."

Ringo leaned to the side and stared behind Billy. "What son of a bitch?" he asked.

Billy whirled around to find no one behind him. "What . . . he was here just a minute ago," he stammered, looking around in the semidarkness.

Ringo glanced down at Billy's empty holster.

"Where's your gun?" he asked.

Billy's hand slapped empty leather. "Why, the bastard must've took it."

Ringo laughed, shaking his head. "Go on home, Billy, 'fore somebody hurts you."

"I tell you he was here," Billy protested.

Ringo's face got sober. "Billy, you're a disgrace to the cowboys. I oughta take that red sash off your waist and strangle you with it."

Chapter 14

Josephine Sarah Marcus Earp kissed Wyatt lightly on the lips, her hand caressing his cheek. "You be careful on your rounds tonight, Wyatt. You know they're probably gunning for you."

Wyatt put his hat on, checked his Colt to make sure it was sitting ready in its holster, and picked up his Winchester rifle. "I'll be careful, Josie, don't you worry none about me. None of those cowboys have the balls to come after me now, not until they see what Judge Spicer's gonna do."

"You keep your guns loose anyway, you hear?"

Wyatt gave her a rueful grin. "Yes, dear. I promise I'll be careful and look both ways before I cross the street."

Josephine shook her head and closed the door as he stepped off the porch.

Sometimes that man is just too stubborn for his own good, she thought as she walked toward the kitchen to clean up the dinner dishes.

She was just putting the last of the dishes in the cupboard when she heard a knock on the door.

"I wonder who that could be?" she muttered as she wiped her hands on her apron to answer the knock.

She opened the door and was surprised to see Sheriff Johnny Behan standing there, his hat in his hand.

"Oh . . . hello, Johnny. What can I do for you?"

"I need to talk to you, Josephine."

She hesitated, then she shook her head. "We don't have anything to say to one another, Johnny. All that's over with now."

Behan reached over and grabbed her by the arm, pulling her out onto the porch. "No, it's not over, Josephine. I brought you out here last year to marry *me*, not that fool Wyatt!"

She jerked her arm out of his grasp and rubbed it with her hand. "I may have come out here intending to marry you, Johnny, but then I met and fell in love with Wyatt. Why can't you just let it be?"

"I ain't never gonna let it be, Josephine," he growled. "Your man's gonna be dead and buried soon, an' then you'll change that tune you're singin."

Josephine's hand flew to her mouth. "What do you mean, Johnny? Do you know something?"

A look of fear crossed Behan's face, as if he'd said too much. "I ain't sayin' nothin' more,

Josephine, but I just wanted you to know it ain't over between us until I say it's over."

A creak of porch boards behind him made Behan turn his head, just in time to be smashed in the face by Morgan Earp's fist.

The blow snapped his head back and split his lip. He stumbled backward, but Morgan followed, swinging from the hip and planting another fist in his stomach, doubling the lawman over. He dropped to his knees.

Morgan stepped up and kicked him in the butt, propelling him off the porch to land facedown in the dirt of the front yard.

As Morgan stood there, his fists balled at his sides, Behan rose clumsily to his feet, sleeved the blood off his mouth and pointed his finger at Morgan. "You're a dead man, Earp, just like your brothers. I'm gonna live to piss on all your graves."

Morgan took a step toward the edge of the porch and Behan spun on his heels and ran away into the night without saying another word.

Josephine came up behind him and put her hand on Morgan's shoulder. "Oh, Morgan. You shouldn't have done that," she said.

"The bastard had it coming, Josie. He had no right talking to another man's wife like that."

She turned him around, her eyes falling to his left shoulder, where a crimson stain was spreading on his white shirt.

"Goodness," she said. "Now look what you've done. You've made your wound go to bleeding again."

A voice called from the darkness in front of the house. "What the hell's goin' on here? I heard shoutin'," Wyatt said as he walked up the steps.

Morgan shook his head. "Nothing, Wyatt. Just a little fracas with that pond scum Behan."

Wyatt glanced up at Josephine. "He botherin' you again, Josie?" he asked, his lips tight and white against the dark tan of his face.

She shook her head. "Not really, Wyatt. But he did say something about someone planning to kill you and your brothers."

Wyatt's face relaxed in his usual, easy grin. "Well, hell, that's not news. Seems like lately anybody wantin' to kill the Earps is gonna have to stand in line."

Morgan gave a short laugh, and Wyatt noticed the blood running down his arm.

"I thought you was gonna have the doc take a look at that."

Morgan shrugged, the movement bringing a wince to his face from the pain. "I was, but the doc was in his cups as usual. He was so drunk he'd probably have stitched up the wrong arm."

Wyatt looked at Josephine. "You gonna be all right while I get Morg taken care of?"

"Sure, Wyatt. I'll lock the door."

"All right. I'm gonna take him over to see that

Doc LeMat at the hotel. He fixed up Doc Holliday's butt right nice the other day."

Leo answered the knock on their hotel room door with his pistol in hand.

"Whoa, there, Doc," Wyatt said, holding up his hands and grinning. "We come in peace."

Leo lowered the pistol. "Come in, Marshal," he said, standing to the side.

Wyatt and Morgan entered the room. Wyatt noticed a painting standing on an easel in the corner. It was covered with a white base paint and there were some charcoal lines that looked suspiciously like his own likeness drawn over the white paint.

Wyatt raised his eyebrows. "Looks like you're startin' on that picture already, Doc."

Leo glanced at the painting he was working on but didn't answer Wyatt's question. "Good evening, Marshal," he said, replacing his LeMat pistol in the shoulder holster he was wearing before stepping into the center of the room. "To what do I owe the pleasure of your company this evening?"

"My brother Morgan's arm is startin' to bleed again, Doc, an' the town doctor is drunker'n a skunk over at the Oriental. We were wonderin' if you might be able to fix it up."

Leo pointed to a couch against a far wall, motioning Morgan to take a seat. "Of course."

He glanced at Wyatt, "Would you bring that

lantern a little closer please? My friend Jacques, who usually assists me in these matters, is for some unknown reason absent this evening."

After he had gotten Morgan to pull his shirt off and lie down, Leo bent over him, examining his shoulder.

"The wound appears to have been torn open recently," he said.

Morgan smiled. "Yeah. I had a little . . . excitement a while ago and it started bleeding again."

"Marshal, would you be so kind as to get my medical bag out of the bedroom? It's the black leather valise on the second shelf in the wardrobe."

Once he had his equipment laid out on a towel on a low table next to the couch, Leo rolled up his sleeves.

"This is going to hurt, Morgan. I don't have any ether or chloroform here in my room to dull the pain."

"That's all right, Doc. Just do what you have to."

Leo took a long straight needle out of his bag and threaded some catgut suture through the eye. "I'll pull the edges together and that should stop the bleeding, but it won't hold if you have any more 'excitement' for the next few days."

"I promise he'll be good, Leo," Wyatt said, "or else I'll be forced to kick his butt like I did when we were kids."

Morgan grinned through gritted teeth as Leo stuck the needle through his skin. "That'll be the day, Wyatt," he said, his voice rough as he fought the pain.

Leo sewed six stitches across the wound, pulling the edges tight to stop the bleeding, then washed the wound with rubbing alcohol, causing Morgan to utter a soft moan.

"There, that should do it, Morgan, unless suppuration sets in. I would like to see you every day so that I can change the bandages and check on the stitching. If the wound begins to get infected, we may have to open it once again."

Morgan looked at Leo. "Then I'll just make damn sure it don't get infected. This was about as much fun as a sharp stick in the eye."

Leo smiled, reaching into his medical bag, pulling out a small brown bottle. "Here's some laudanum. Take two teaspoons every three or four hours for the pain, but do not drink alcohol with it."

Morgan took the bottle and took a deep draught, screwing up his face at the bitter taste.

Wyatt stuck out his hand. "It seems once again I'm in your debt, Doc LeMat."

Leo shook Wyatt's hand. "It is nothing, Marshal. Agreeing to sit for my portrait is payment enough."

Wyatt put his hat back on his head and helped

Morgan to his feet. "I've got to finish my rounds," he said. "We'll see you tomorrow, Leo."

"Good evening, Marshal," Leo said, moving over to the door. "If you happen to see my friend Jacques wandering around, would you tell him it's time for him to come home?"

Wyatt grinned. "Certainly, Leo. You take it easy now, you hear?"

After the two men left, Leo walked to the window of the room and pulled the drapes back. He stood there, looking out over the town of Tombstone, which even though the hour was late seemed to be every bit as busy as during the day.

He thought over the current situation, wondering how he and Jacques might best help the marshal and his brothers in their current difficulties.

As he considered their options, he also worried about where Jacques might be at this late hour. It was unlike him to take off on his own without letting Leo know where he was going.

Leo hoped his friend was not doing something they would both regret later. He didn't relish trying to explain to the authorities why Jacques would cut someone's throat who had merely mentioned the possibility of an attack on Leo.

Chapter 15

"My ear!" Curly Bill Brocius screamed, staring at his face in front of a mirror at Barker's Boarding House, where he rented a room by the week. "That little bastard cut off the top of my goddamn ear!"

Ike Clanton stood behind Curly Bill. Dried blood covered the left side of Curly Bill's cheek, and the top of his left ear was cut off in a straight line, raw red meat looking sore and ragged.

"Who was he?" Ike asked. "Before we go after somebody we gotta know who done it."

Curly Bill's jaw jutted out defiantly. "He didn't give me his goddamn name! It was some little son of a bitch with a scar on his face. He wore a white cap of some kind an' was dressed all in black. He spoke some damn foreign words to me. I ain't never heard 'em before. Wasn't Spanish. I'm real sure of that."

"The sailor," Ike said. "He's with LeMat. I

heard about him when they came into town. Got a long scar down one of his cheeks."

"That's him," Curly Bill said. "I'm gonna find him and kill him. Look at my goddamn ear! The top part of it's plumb gone. He snuck up behind me or I'd have filled him with lead. He got the drop on me when I wasn't lookin'."

"Him and LeMat are stayin' at the Cosmopolitan Hotel. Only, he ain't gonna be easy to kill on account of this LeMat. LeMat claims to be a doctor, but he carries a gun under his coat an' he's a friend of the Earps. Doc Holliday, too. Somebody at the Red Dog said that LeMat was a hired shootist. That's why he's in Tombstone. He came here to kill somebody, only nobody's sure who he's after. He tells the story that he's a painter of pictures, but that's just a cover. He ain't nothin' but an assassin, an' the little guy who's with him figures to be a back-shooter of some kind. He don't look like no gun for hire."

"The little bastard," Curly Bill spat. "What the hell is his name?"

"I ain't sure," Ike replied, "but I can find out. All I know is that he came here with LeMat."

"Find out what room he's stayin' in at the Cosmopolitan. I'm gonna put him under. Nobody can do this to a cowboy. The little son of a bitch took my sash off and tied it around my neck, like it was a damn joke!"

Ike watched Curly Bill apply wintergreen ointment to the top of his ear, wincing at the pain it caused when he rubbed it into the open edges of the cut. "You're right, Curly Bill. We can't let 'em get away with this. I'll round up Ned and a couple more boys soon as I find out who the little foreigner is. We'll shoot him soon as we're ready. All we gotta do is find him an' get him in the right spot so there ain't no witnesses."

"Damn right we'll kill him," Curly Bill growled, wincing when he touched his ear with a fingertip. "Only we ain't gonna shoot him. Once we git the drop on him, whilst you and Ned cover him, I'm gonna take my skinnin' knife and gut the sumbitch like a deer carcass. Then we'll leave him hangin' on a post for that fancy-pants friend of his to find. Nobody comes to Tombstone to ride roughshod over a cowboy. He threatened me. He said he'd cut off my head an' put it in front of Earp's office, like I was a goddamn pig at butcherin' time. Ain't no son of a bitch gonna talk to a cowboy like that in this town. We gotta teach him an' that doctor a lesson."

"Like you said, it's real simple, Curly Bill. We just kill the mangy coyote an' be done with him," Ike said. "I'll get word to Ringo, the Baxter boys, and Billy, too. We find out what room he's in an' then we just go upstairs and cut him up real good. Behan won't say a word, an' Virgil, along with Morgan, are shot up pretty bad. The only feller we gotta worry about is Wyatt. And that doctor with the gun."

"We'll kill him, too," Curly Bill snapped. "Damn, my ear smarts something fierce!"

"Maybe it'll grow back," Ike said. "Hell, there's just a little piece of it gone."

Curly Bill whirled around, wiping dried blood from his face. He stared into Ike's eyes for a moment. "You're dumb as a damn rock, Ike," he said. "A man's ear don't grow back. I'm gonna look like this the rest of my life, an' all on account of that little sawed-off runt in the sailor's cap. Just find out who he is, and what room he's in at the hotel. If that fancy-pants doctor gets in the way, I'll gut him, too."

"By the way, Curly Bill, Ringo told me he was gonna call in all the cowboys from around the county to come to Tombstone."

Curly Bill looked surprised. "Oh?"

"Yeah. Ringo says the Earps're gittin' too big fer their britches. He figgers if we git some reinforcements in town, we can take 'em down a notch or two."

Curly Bill's face turned dark. "You mean he don't think we're up to it ourselves?"

Ike's voice took on a placating tone. "That ain't it, Curly Bill. It's just that after that fracas at the O.K. Corral the other week, he thinks we need more guns."

Curly Bill's lips turned up in a sneer. "Yeah,

well, if a couple'a the men hadn't turned tail and run away, the outcome of the fight might've been a mite different."

Ike's face blushed a deep crimson. "Hell, Curly Bill, it weren't like that an' you know it. Virgil Earp took my pistol and Winchester away from me and buffaloed me with his pistol barrel. My guns was at the Grand Hotel when the fight commenced or I'd've joined right in."

Curly Bill glared at Ike. "I also heard some rumors to the fact that Wyatt Earp offered you the six-thousand-dollar reward for helpin' him capture Bill Leonard, Jim Crane, and Harry Head after they robbed that Benson stage."

Ike's face blanched pure white and his eyes flickered, unable to meet Curly Bill's. "Who tole you that bald-faced lie?" he mumbled, looking at his boots.

"Word is, some folks heard you discussin' it with Wyatt over at the Red Dog . . . somethin' 'bout you bein' pissed off 'cause Wyatt told a Wells Fargo agent named Marshall Williams about your deal for the reward money."

"It ain't true, Curly Bill, I swear it!" Ike pleaded, grabbing Curly Bill's vest with both hands.

Curly Bill brushed Ike's hands away, a contemptuous look alighting on his face. "It'd better not be, Ike, or you'll wind up hangin' from the same post as that little sailor man."

* * *

Jacques entered his room. It was close to dawn and he was sure Leo would be asleep, but the connecting door between their rooms was open and a lantern was lit.

"Where've you been?" Leo asked, brushing a coat of white base paint across a canvas on his easel.

"I could not sleep," Jacques lied, closing the door behind him.

"Nothing like a walk in the fresh night air to put a man's mind to rest," Leo said, giving Jacques a sideways glance. "I would've ventured a guess that some young woman was involved, but I see blood all over your pants. Surely you didn't have to cut the fair maiden's throat in order to seduce her?"

Jacques looked down at his pants leg. Blood from Curly Bill's ear was all over his right leg and boot. "I . . . met with some misfortune near one of the saloons. It is nothing to worry about. Someone tried to rob me."

"You're a bad liar, old friend," Leo said without taking his eyes off the canvas he was preparing for Earp's portrait. "Why don't you tell me about it?"

Jacques sighed, slumping against the door frame. "You know me too well."

At that, Leo smiled. "You're a bad-tempered

Cajun from the slums of New Orleans. What else is there to say?"

"I cut off the tip of a man's ear."

"I'm sure you had a reason to take such a drastic measure. Did the scoundrel impugn your culinary skills, perhaps?"

"He was one of the men plotting to kill you and Wyatt Earp."

"And what's this man with one ear's name?"

Jacques frowned and waved a dismissive hand. "I didn't cut the entire ear off, just a small piece to get his attention and teach him a lesson." He thought for a moment, then added, "They called him Curly Bill, as I remember. He was wearing one of the red sashes around his belly. He is one of those pigs who call themselves cowboys. I was in the Red Dog Saloon when I overheard their conversation. I told you about it."

"You didn't kill him?" Leo asked.

"No. I only gave him a slight warning to leave Earp alone, and to stay away from you."

Leo chuckled. "I appreciate your concern for my welfare, but it'd be best, as I told you before, if we stayed out of this local squabble."

"He was plotting to kill you, *mon ami*."

Leo added more white to the base paint he was using. "Men have tried before. I'm still alive."

"There were four of them at the table when I heard them talking."

"My uncle's revolver holds more than four bullets."

"I only warned this man to stay away from you—"

"And you cut off his ear at the same time?"

"A part of it, as I said. I wanted him to know I was serious about what I was telling him."

"It seems a bit extreme, Jacques. Your bad temper got the best of you, like that time when we were children playing on the docks when you beat a man half to death for making fun of your young friend from the upper crust of New Orleans society."

"Perhaps."

Leo took a deep breath. "I think it's best that we leave these cowboys alone. We didn't come all this way to become involved in local politics. I intend to paint Wyatt Earp's portrait, and possibly Doc Holliday's. He's an interesting character. Then we'll go back to Tucson and board the first train to San Antonio."

"I have a feeling it will not be that easy," Jacques told him. "Trouble seems to follow you wherever we go. I am going to sleep for a few hours. Wake me up if you need me for anything."

Leo chuckled as he stroked his brush across the canvas. "Certainly. If a man who's wearing a red sash and has only one ear comes to the door, I'll awaken you so you can cut the other one off to make a matched set."

Jacques hesitated, started to reply, then shook his head and proceeded into his bedroom.

After he left the room, the smile faded from Leo's face as he considered what Jacques had told him. Perhaps it was time to take a stand in the feud after all. It was plain to see that the Earps, for all their faults, were trying to make Tombstone more civilized, and who could argue with that?

Jacques appeared in his bedroom doorway, dressed for bed. "Good night, Leo."

Leo glanced up. "By the way, Jacques. Marshal Wyatt brought his brother Morgan by the hotel tonight."

"Oh?"

"Yes. It seems he got into a fight and tore the wound on his left shoulder open. I had to stitch it up again."

"Does it appear to be healing properly?"

Leo shrugged. "Some slight signs of infection, but overall I should think he will be all right sooner rather than later."

Jacques snapped his fingers. "Oh, I almost forgot to tell you, Leo. While I was sitting at a nearby table to the gunmen, I heard them say they were going to meet tomorrow night at the China Tiger for another meeting to plan how to kill you and the Earps."

Leo stroked his chin thoughtfully. "Then, by all means, perhaps we should pay a visit to this China Tiger and see what transpires at that meeting."

Jacques nodded, the scar on his cheek pulling his lips into a savage grin when he understood what Leo intended to do.

Chapter 16

Leo stepped through the batwings of Campbell and Hatch's Saloon just after eight o'clock in the morning, followed by a complaining Jacques.

"I don't know why you insist on eating breakfast in a saloon," Jacques said with a scowl on his face. "The food in this godforsaken place is bad enough in the so-called best restaurants without patronizing barrooms for our meals."

Leo shook his head. "Sometimes you amaze me. I would think a judge of fine cuisine would always be on the lookout for a chance to try something new, or different."

"New and different is one thing, while new and tasteless is something I can do without. Food in this part of the world has no character."

As Leo walked toward the dining section, he caught sight of Doc Holliday sitting in a corner with four other cowboys playing poker. Doc looked as if he'd been up all night. His face was the color of old parchment and had a slick sheen of sweat on it, while his eyes were sunken and muddy. A half-empty bottle of whiskey sat at his elbow and he was drinking from a tin cup.

A woman sat on the arm of his chair, her arm draped across his shoulders, a concerned look on her face. Although not pretty in the classical sense, with thin lips, a weak chin, and a nose slightly too large for her features, it was obvious she cared about Doc, for she continually caressed the back of his neck with her hand.

Leo walked over to the table. "Good morning, Doc," he said, tipping his hat.

Doc looked up through bleary eyes, his lips curling slightly in his trademark half smile. "Why, good morning, Doctor," he said, nodding. His eyes shifted to Jacques. "Hello, Jacques. How are you this fine day?"

Jacques grinned crookedly. "So far, Doc, I'm fine, but I haven't yet partaken of the breakfast Leo has planned for us. After that, I'm sure I will be in bed for the rest of the week recovering."

Doc glanced down at his cards, shrugged, and tossed them onto the table. He stood up, staggering just a moment as he was overcome by a bout of dizziness. "This is your lucky day, gentlemen," he stated to the other players. "I'm going to leave you with the remainder of your money while I have breakfast with my friends."

He put his arm around the woman's shoulders

and followed Leo and Jacques to a table in the dining room.

After they were seated, Doc said, "Dr. Leo LeMat and Jacques LeDieux, I'd like you to meet my favorite lady, Kate Elder."

Leo and Jacques nodded and said hello, as did Kate.

"How long were you playing poker, Doc?" Leo asked as their plump waitress poured coffee all around.

Kate gave Doc a hard look. "He's been sitting there for hours," she replied.

Leo shook his head. "You know that isn't good for your wound, Doc. You need bed rest."

Doc waved a dismissive hand and signaled the waitress. "Ma'am, bring me a little brandy to sweeten up this coffee."

"You've had enough, Doc," Kate said.

Doc's eyes turned hard as he glared at her. "Don't be telling me what to do and not do, Kate. I'm still thirsty for distilled spirits."

She jumped up from the table, tears in her eyes. "Why do I waste my breath!" she said with some feeling. "Go ahead and kill yourself. You seem determined to do it. No matter what I say." She stormed out of the room.

Doc looked after her with sympathetic eyes. "Poor Kate. She thinks she's taken me to raise."

"She seems to care very much for you, Doc," Jacques said, his eyes on her retreating form.

"She does. Too much, I think at times."

"How did you two meet?" Leo asked.

"That's a funny story," Doc said, taking a bottle of brandy from the waitress and pouring a generous portion into his coffee. He took a sip, smiled his approval, and lit a long black cigar. Leo had to restrain himself from telling Doc that smoking was the worst thing he could do with his tuberculosis.

"I was playing cards over at Fort Griffin with a man named Bailey. I caught him cheating and warned him to play his poker straight. Well, when I won the next pot, Bailey went for his gun. He wasn't very fast and I had time to plant a knife in his brisket."

He took a deep drag from his cigar, coughed violently for a moment, then resumed his story.

"A little later, I was just escorting Miss Elder up to my room at the hotel when the town marshal and two of his deputies cornered me in the lobby. I could hear a crowd of citizens outside shouting something about a necktie party." He chuckled. "Miss Kate slipped out the door, tied a couple of horses out behind the hotel, and set fire to a nearby shed. She came running into the lobby shouting, 'Fire! Fire!' and whilst the lawmen were distracted, she pulled an old Colt Army pistol out and got the drop on them. We lit out of town and we've been together ever since."

Both Leo and Jacques laughed appreciatively.

"That sounds like a good woman to have on your side, Doc," Leo said.

The smile left Doc's face. "Yeah, she is, and I'm damned if I know why I treat her so bad."

"Every man has his own demons inside, Doc " Leo said. "And every day is a battle between the man and his dark side." Leo shrugged. "Some days, the demons win and we behave badly, while on other days, we win and behave honorably." He nodded at the brandy sitting next to Doc on the table. "That stuff seems to give demons the edge."

Doc's eyes brightened a little. "You're right, Leo, but hell, Kate can down this firewater fastern'n I can. Maybe that's our problem."

The discussion was interrupted by the arrival of their breakfast.

After they finished their meal, Leo and Jacques walked down the boardwalk toward their hotel.

"What did you think of the food, Jacques?" Leo asked.

"I now know why westerners call their biscuits 'sinkers,'" Jacques replied, rubbing his stomach. "They sank to the bottom of my gullet, sitting there reminding me never to eat at Campbell and Hatch's again. I feel like I swallowed a cannonball."

Leo started to reply when he saw two men slip into an alleyway ahead of them. "Did you see that, Jacques?" he asked, inclining his head toward the alley.

"*Oui*, Leo. The men were wearing the red sashes of the cowboy gang."

Leo reached inside his coat and loosened his Baby LeMat revolver in its holster, while Jacques slipped his Arkansas toothpick stiletto out of his boot and into his belt.

When they came abreast of the alley, Billy Claiborne and a young man Leo did not recognize stepped out.

Claiborne had a gun in his hand hanging down at his side. He glanced around the street to make sure no one was watching, then he growled, "Hey, mister. We don't appreciate no strangers comin' into our town and causin' trouble."

Claiborne was a big man, about five feet ten inches tall with a barrel chest and thick, muscular arms. Leo recognized him as a bully type who probably started fights with just about anyone as long as they were smaller than he was.

The boy added, "Yeah. So why don't you just get back on your hosses and hightail it on outta here?"

Leo glanced at Jacques, a slight smile on his face. "Do you feel like leaving town, Jacques?" he asked mildly.

Jacques, whose eyes never left the two men in front of them wagged his head. "No," he said simply.

Leo looked back at Claiborne and the youth.

"I don't either," Leo said evenly.

"We ain't exactly askin'. We're tellin' you to leave," Billy said, flexing his muscles and sticking his chest out, the gun moving up to point at Leo's waist.

Leo made a half turn toward Jacques, as if to say something to him, and suddenly his LeMat pistol appeared in his hand, cocked and aimed at Claiborne's nose.

"Excuse me," Leo said. "I don't think I heard you."

Claiborne swallowed with an audible gulp and dropped his pistol in the dirt. "Don't go for no gun, Baxter," he said.

Leo shook his head. "Just as I thought. A coward, like all bullies.

Baxter's hand went to the butt of his pistol, but before he could clear leather, Jacques had the point of his knife against his throat. "Perhaps you would like a taste of iron?" he asked.

Baxter's eyes widened and he held his hand out from his side. "I don't want no trouble, mister," he croaked through a dry throat.

Leo glanced at Jacques. "These cowboys are determined to make our stay in Tombstone miserable," he said.

Jacques grinned. "I do believe it would enhance their memories the next time they are tempted to interfere with us, Leo, if we gave them something to think about."

Leo holstered his pistol, took his hat off and hung it on the end of a hitching rail as he stepped into the street.

"Well, Billy," he said as he pulled a pair of leather riding gloves on, looking as if he were preparing to fight Billy hand-to-hand. "Would you like to make me leave town? If so, let's settle this like gentlemen."

Billy licked his lips, his small piggish eyes darting around to see if there was any way out of this. Finally, he rolled up his sleeves, revealing hairy, muscular arms. "You're gonna regret this, LeMat."

"Are you sure you want to do this, Billy? I don't particularly want to spread your nose all over your face. It's already ugly enough."

The big man growled and came running at Leo, swinging his right hand in a roundhouse punch.

Leo set his feet and didn't move, merely leaning his head slightly to the side so Claiborne's blow whistled harmlessly by his face.

As Claiborne twisted sideways from the force of his swing, Leo threw a short left jab into his ribs, cracking one with a snap like a brittle wooden stick.

Claiborne grabbed his side, bent over, and let out his breath with a giant groan.

While he stood there, Leo swung a right uppercut from his heels, catching Claiborne flush on the bridge of his nose. Blood and teeth went flying as Claiborne's head snapped back and he staggered upright.

He stood there in the middle of the street, swaying and shaking his head, trying to uncross his eyes, blood streaming from his ruined nose. He spat two more teeth from between split lips and howled in anger as he ran at Leo once more, his arms spread wide as if to catch him in a bear hug.

Leo bent under the cowboy's arms and threw two quick jabs into Claiborne's paunch, doubling him over. The big man stood there, leaning over with his hands on his knees, and began to vomit onto his boots.

Leo stepped back, his face a mask of disgust as he turned to Baxter. "Do you want some of this fight?"

"No . . . no, sir!" Baxter said, his nose wrinkling at the hideous smell coming from his friend.

"Good. Then I trust we won't have any more foolishness from you boys?" Leo said as he removed his gloves.

"No, sir," Baxter said in a low voice, his eyes not meeting Leo's.

Jacques handed Leo his hat and they walked off.

"I cannot believe you risked injury to your hands like that," Jacques said while Leo straightened his hat.

"That's why I made sure only to hit him in his softer parts," Leo replied, rubbing bruised knuckles, "although his nose was harder than I thought."

Behind them, Baxter watched them walk off. He was momentarily tempted to draw his gun and shoot them in the back. Then he remembered how lightning fast LeMat was with that pistol and how deadly the Frenchman's eyes looked. His hand relaxed and he bent over Billy.

He patted his back as the man continued to retch and vomit.

"You all right, Billy?" he asked.

Billy turned bloodshot eyes up at his young friend. "Of course I'm not all right, you idiot!" he snapped, then groaned as the effort sent tongues of fire through his chest from his fractured ribs.

"That bastard broke me up inside. Help me up. I gotta go see the doctor."

"You think we oughta tell Ringo what happened first?" Baxter asked, looking over his shoulder at the retreating figures of LeMat and his crazy companion.

"Hell with Ringo," Billy growled. "I think I'm dyin' here. Get me up on my feet an' help me get to the doc's place."

Baxter bent over and put his arms around Billy's chest, causing him to cry out in pain.

"Not so hard," Billy cried. "I'm hurt real bad."

Chapter 17

Leo and Jacques were resting in their hotel room, enjoying chicory coffee, when a knock came at the door.

Jacques picked up his shotgun, Ange, before opening the door. Wyatt Earp, his hat in his hand, stood there with a worried look on his face.

"Howdy, Jacques. I need to see Doc LeMat," he said.

"Certainly, Marshal Earp. Come in," Jacques said, stepping aside.

"Hello, Marshal Earp," Leo said, rising from his chair. "Would you care for some chicory coffee?"

Earp shook his head. "No, thanks. I'm afraid I've come to ask you yet another favor."

Leo nodded. "Anything within my power, Wyatt."

"My brother, Virgil, took a shot to the right calf in the shoot-out, an' the wound's looking pretty bad." He twisted his hat and it was plain to Leo that Wyatt was a man not accustomed to asking for favors. "Would you mind taking a look at it?" Wyatt asked.

"Of course. Jacques, would you get my bag?"

The three men walked down Main Street to the Lincoln Hotel, where Virgil and his wife had a room.

When they entered, Morgan and his wife, Louisa, were standing next to a bed holding Virgil, while Virgil's wife, Allie, and Wyatt's wife, Josie, stood on the other side.

Leo smiled and took off his hat.

His smile faded when he glanced at Virgil. His face was flushed and covered with a fine sheen of sweat, and Leo could see by the pulsations in his throat that his heart was beating very rapidly— not a good sign for a man with a bullet wound.

Leo stepped to the side of the bed and gently pulled the covers down. Dark bloodstains covered the bandage around the wound to his leg, and the smell of putrification that arose from his injury was overpowering in the small room.

Leo straightened up, and as he began to remove his coat, he looked at the women. "Perhaps the ladies would like to adjourn to the sitting room while I work?"

"Of course, Doctor," Morgan's wife said. "Come on, Allie, Josie. Let's go fix some coffee for the men."

Virgil's eyes narrowed in pain as he struggled to rise to a sitting position to get a better look at his leg. "How bad is it, Doc?" he asked, his voice husky and hoarse from his obvious fever.

Leo shook his head. "Not good, Virgil. It appears as if gangrene has set in." Leo hesitated. "Perhaps you've been walking on it too much. I noticed the other day you were doing quite a bit of moving around the town on your crutches."

Virgil nodded. "I can't let Wyatt and Morg do all the work, 'specially with Morg's arm bein' wounded and all."

"Well, you're certainly going to have to stay off your feet for a while now. This is a very serious complication," Leo said as he sat on the edge of the bed.

Virgil's expression fell and he slumped back against the pillows piled at the head of the bed. "That mean you're gonna have to take it off?"

Leo thought for a moment. "That would certainly be the most prudent thing to do."

Virgil shook his head. "No! I'd rather die than live as a cripple."

Leo shrugged. "There are a couple of other things we might try."

"What?" Wyatt asked.

"A physician named John Hunter wrote a book called *A Treatise on the Blood, Inflammation, and Gunshot Wounds* in 1794. He advocated applications of bark and bleeding of the area around the wound by attaching leeches in cases like this."

"Leeches?" Morgan asked, his expression bewildered.

Leo nodded.

Wyatt shook his head. "I'm afraid we don't have none of those around here, Doc.

Leo pursed his lips. "I've never particularly agreed with that recommendation anyway. There is one other thing we could try."

"What's that, Doc? I'll do anything to keep my leg," Virgil said, his face showing a glimmer of hope for the first time since Leo entered the room.

"An army doctor named D. J. Larrey wrote about such wounds in his book *Memoirs of Military Surgery* in 1814. He stated that in suppurated wounds in Syria, he'd noted they often found worms, or larvae of blue flies, growing in the decaying flesh."

"Larvae?" Wyatt asked. "You mean maggots?"

"Through extensive study, Dr. Larrey found that though the insects were troublesome to the patients, they expedited the healing of the wounds by shortening the work of nature and causing the sloughs to fall off."

"What's that mean in English, Doc?" Morgan said, his brow furrowed, his eyes flicking toward Virgil as if to gauge how he was taking the idea of putting maggots in his wound.

"It means the maggots ate the dead and decaying flesh, while not bothering the good flesh, and thus they caused the wound to heal faster and more completely than it would have otherwise."

"But where are we gonna get maggots?" Wyatt asked. "Makes me kind of sick thinkin' about it."

Leo bent over his doctor's bag and withdrew a small jar, which he handed to Jacques. "Take this to the alleyways behind the restaurants in town, Jacques. Look in the garbage piles for pieces of old meat. I'm sure you won't have any trouble finding a suitable supply of small maggots."

Jacques smiled. "So long as the maggots do not care overly much about the quality of the meat they are eating."

Wyatt grabbed his hat. "Come on, Jacques. I've never heard of such a thing, but if the doc says it'll help Virge keep his leg, then I'll help you look."

An hour later, Wyatt and Jacques returned with a jar full of small, wiggling, white worm larvae. "Is this enough, Leo?" Jacques asked.

"That should do," Leo replied, taking a pair of forceps from his bag.

He carefully picked out dozens of the small maggots and placed them within the wound, among the blackened, rotting tissue.

He watched carefully as they burrowed deeper until they were almost out of sight in the pus and old blood.

"It won't hurt none, will it?" Morgan asked.

Leo shook his head. "No, as I said before, the

larvae only eat the dead tissue that has no feeling. They will not eat meat that is alive and healthy."

"Doc," Wyatt said, "do me a favor. Don't mention none of this to the womenfolk." He smiled grimly, glancing toward the door to the sitting room. "Being of a more sensitive nature, they might not understand puttin' maggot worms in Virge's leg."

Leo laughed softly. "I agree." He glanced down at Virgil. "Keep the wound lightly covered with a bandage, not too tight, and stay off your feet. It'll make it easier for the . . . animals to do their work."

Virgil nodded. "And if this don't do the trick?"

"Then, my friend, we'll have no choice but to remove the leg at the knee."

Wyatt bent over and smoothed the hair off Virgil's forehead. "It'll work, big brother," he said in a gentle voice.

Virgil shook his head. "If it don't, Wyatt, just leave me in a room with my Colt handy. I don't intend to spend the rest of my life hobblin' around on one leg."

Leo stepped into the room where the wives were gathered. He addressed Virgil's wife, Allie.

"I want you to keep Virgil as quiet as possible, Mrs. Earp," he said. "I realize there is quite a bit of excitement concerning the brothers right now, but for Virgil's sake, try to keep him out of it as much as possible."

Allie nodded. "What else, Doctor?"

"He needs plenty of fluids, especially water. His leg is badly infected and will cause him to have fever and night sweats, all of which deprive the body of water. He also needs a diet rich in meat . . . heavy beef broth, steak if he can keep it down, beef stew if he can't—food such as that."

"That won't be any problem, Dr. LeMat," Morgan's wife, Lou, said, stepping to Allie's side and putting her hand on her shoulder. "Josie and I will help fetch whatever Virgil needs to get better. Since we've moved here to stay together and be safe, we have no cooking facilities."

Morgan stepped forward. "I could talk to Bea over at the boarding house, doc. She can fix up whatever you say and we can bring it here for Virgil to eat."

Leo nodded. "Remember, the most important thing over the next week or two is for him to get as much rest as possible."

When everyone nodded their agreement, Leo picked up his hat and he and Jacques left the room.

As they walked down the street toward their hotel, Jacques asked, "What do you think his chances are, Leo?"

Leo glanced back over his shoulders and grinned. "In anyone else, I'd say not very good. But with these Earp brothers, who knows? They are all remarkable men."

Chapter 18

It was just after nine o'clock in the morning and Jacques and Leo were finishing their breakfast in the Cosmopolitan Hotel's dining room. Jacques leaned back in his chair and wiped his mouth with the linen napkin he'd stuffed down the front of his shirt.

"*Mon Dieu*," he said with a sigh. "Either the food in this rat hole of a town is getting better, or my taste buds are withering away from lack of stimulation."

Leo nodded, glancing at a menu left on the table. "You know, Jacques, the former name for Tombstone was Goose Creek, and yet nowhere on any of the menus in this town have I seen either duck or goose being served."

Jacques laughed, pulling his napkin out of his shirt and wadding it into a ball. "That is most probably because the geese, like this old Cajun, could find nothing even remotely worth eating in this region and left for parts north."

Leo smiled at his friend's constant complaining as a young boy walked to deliver a handwritten note.

Leo gave him a coin and unfolded the message. "I wonder what this is all about," he said, passing the paper across the table to Jacques.

Jacques read it aloud: "The members of the Citizen's Safety Committee request the honor of a meeting with you at Hafford's Saloon."

"Have you heard of this committee before, Leo?"

Leo shook his head. "No, but I suppose I'll see what they want."

When they cautiously entered Hafford's Saloon, they found a table at the back of the room occupied by a number of men, most of whom were wearing business suits, though a few had the look of hardened gunfighters about them.

Leo and Jacques walked over to the table. "I am Dr. Leo LeMat, and this is my associate, Jacques LeDieux."

A portly man with graying hair and a large mustache with muttonchop sideburns rose, extending his hand. "I'm Mayor John Clum, head of the Citizen's Safety Committee."

After they shook hands, he turned to the table and pointed to the rough-looking men one by one. "There on the end is Turkey Creek Jack Johnson, next to him is Texas Jack Vermillion and Sherman McMasters.

"On the other side of the table are Vincent Boyle and Samuel Goodson," Clum added, indicating men dressed in more conservative business attire.

After the introductions were over, Clum held out his palm. "Please have a seat and let me explain why we've asked you here today."

Once they were seated, and coffee and small snifters of brandy were served all around, Clum got right to the point. "The Citizen's Safety Committee is a group of businessmen and ranchers who are interested in seeing Tombstone grow and prosper, and in halting the activities of a group of men calling themselves cowboys."

Leo nodded, not saying anything until he saw the lay of the land.

"As such, we've always supported the Earp brothers, who've been good for business and helped keep the lawlessness to a bare minimum," Clum went on.

"And have your feelings now changed?" Leo asked.

"Oh, no. As a matter of fact, that's why we asked to meet with you. Lately, since the gunfight at the O.K. Corral, Johnny Ringo and Ike Clanton have been calling in all of their cowboy friends from the out-country. I gather you've noticed the sudden influx of men wearing red sashes around their waists?"

Leo glanced at Jacques. They'd discussed that very fact this morning at breakfast, wondering if it spelled trouble for Wyatt and his brothers.

Clum reached into his vest pocket and pulled out a parchment card, which he placed on the table in front of Leo. It read, "Portraitist. Gun for Hire," and it had Leo's name at the bottom of it in dark black ink.

"Ned Boyle, Vincent's brother, is bartender over at the Oriental, and Doc Holliday gave him your card."

Leo didn't reply, but he continued looking at Clum, waiting for him to get to the point.

"This committee, as I said, supports the Earps, and in view of the fact that they're soon to be greatly outnumbered, we'd like to hire you and your associate to . . . watch out for them. Your card says your gun is for hire, and we've been told you are skilled in the use of it."

Leo frowned. Why was it, he thought, that men had trouble stating what they really meant when it came to violence? "By that, I take it to mean you'd like Jacques and me to do whatever is necessary to make sure the cowboys don't get the upper hand here in Tombstone?" Leo asked, pushing the card back across the table toward Clum.

Clum nodded, grinning when he saw Leo knew exactly what he was after.

Leo questioned the wisdom of allowing his dark side to interfere with his primary objective; that of painting Wyatt Earp, and perhaps a portrait of Doc Holliday. But unless he took steps to ensure Wyatt's safety, no portrait could be done.

"Jacques and I both have sympathies ourselves for what the Earps are trying to do here in Tombstone, so I might accept an offer of employment."

"And what's gonna be your fee?" Turkey Creek Jack Johnson asked around a cigar stuck in the corner of his mouth.

Leo considered it for a moment. "Five hundred dollars," Leo responded.

"That's mighty steep!" Texas Jack said, a look of disgust on his face.

Leo glanced at the pistol on Texas Jack's hip. "You're wearing a sidearm, Mr. Vermillion. You're welcome to take the job, and my friend and I will not be offended in the least."

Texas Jack sat back, his face flushing red. "No . . . no, that's all right. From what I hear, you're an expert at this, so it's probably better left to you. Here's your badge. You can get one for Mr. LeDieux at the city marshal's office."

"As you wish," Leo said, taking the badge before coming to his feet. "The initial retainer may be delivered to me at the Cosmopolitan Hotel." He tipped his hat. "One more thing I need from you, gentlemen. I want a vote on a city ordinance that it will be against the law to wear a red sash around your waist in Tombstone."

"That's gonna be hard to enforce," Mayor Clum said, "but you got my vote on it. How about the rest of you?" he asked the men at the table. "Raise your hands if you're in favor of an ordinance prohibiting the wearing of red sashes."

All hands went up, albeit some of them slowly.

"It's done," Clum said.

"We'll begin at once," Leo said, turning for the door.

Jacques hesitated, then upended his brandy glass, wiped his lips with the back of his hand, and followed Leo out of the saloon.

When they were fifty feet down the boardwalk, Jacques asked, "Leo, would you mind telling me why you have done this thing?"

Leo smiled. "The money will more than cover our expenses in Tombstone. In case you've forgotten, making a living is sometimes a necessary evil."

"But you have plenty of money," Jacques protested. "And the cowboys I overheard in the Red Dog were plotting to kill you, as well as Marshal Earp."

"I came here to paint Wyatt Earp's portrait. Until my canvas is finished I'd do anything within my power to protect him, if the need arises. May as well get paid for it."

"I should have slit Curly Bill's throat when I had the chance," Jacques muttered. "I had the advantage." He gazed up at Leo. "There are times when I forget."

"Forget what?" Leo asked.

"What is written on your business card . . . that your gun as well as your paintbrush is for hire."

Leo pinned the city marshal's badge to his lapel.

"Look at it this way, Jacques," Leo explained. "These so-called cowboys are already gunning for us, as you so readily found out. If they do come after us, as I suspect they will when they've received ample help from the men they've asked to come to town, we will in any case need to defend ourselves."

He shrugged and smiled, though there was very little warmth in the smile. "So as I said before, if we're bound to be drawn into this war between the Earps and the cowboys, why not get paid for it?"

Jacques nodded. "And I do kind of like the idea of men paying us to do the work they want done but are too . . . afraid to do themselves."

Leo adjusted the badge so it hung straight and walked down the street.

"When will I get my badge?" Jacques asked, following.

"Right now, *mon ami*," Leo said, walking toward the city marshal's office.

Chapter 19

Henry Stanley settled into a chair in Cochise County Sheriff Behan's office. He had been to the office of John Clum, editor of the *Tombstone Epitaph*, after talking about the showdown at the O.K. Corral with the editor of the *Tombstone Nugget*, a rival newspaper with strong ties to the Democratic party and the Territorial government in Prescott and Pima County. Clum had described Wyatt Earp as "my ideal of the strong, manly, serious and capable peace officer."

"I hear you're a famous reporter," Behan said. "You found that feller . . . the doctor, over in Africa."

"It was mostly luck," Stanley said, "although it was a most difficult journey. I came to Tombstone to find out the truth about this incident at the O.K. Corral. I understand City Marshal Virgil Earp is seriously wounded. I have the names of the others who died. What started all this? I've been told there is some sort of rebel faction in the county calling themselves the cowboys, and that they wear red sashes."

"I wouldn't call them a rebel faction," Behan said. "The Earps might be considered the rebels. When the shooting was over, three of the cowboys were dead and two Earp brothers were wounded. Also the hired killer Doc Holliday, a most unsavory character with some sort of lung disease, took a bullet in the hip. I attempted to disarm them after the shooting, however they refused to surrender their guns."

"Mr. Clum over at the newspaper office told me that twenty-seven shots were fired in less than half a minute."

Behan nodded. "I went down to the O.K. Corral to try to disarm the cowboys, the Clantons, Tom and Frank McLaury. Ike was staggering drunk. They all refused to lay down their arms. Being so badly outnumbered, there was nothing I could do."

"Who fired the first shot?" Stanley asked.

"Some say it was Wyatt. Others insist Billy Clanton fired first. No one is quite sure. On the evening of October the twenty-fifth, while taking in the town with his friend Tom McLaury, Ike Clanton bucked the tiger, playing faro in a saloon on Allen Street. About eleven that night, drunk as a fiddler, he walked into the Alhambra Lunch Counter for a bite to eat. He had the misfortune to run into Doc. Words were exchanged. Doc slapped Ike across the face and might have killed him right then, until Morgan Earp intervened and pulled Holliday outside to cool off. More threats were tossed back and forth between Clanton and Holliday. Then Ike braced Wyatt in front of the Eagle Brewery and told him that in the morning, they would meet man to man. Wyatt is a U.S. deputy marshal and he took no guff from Ike, or anyone else. As you know, the next day they met at the O.K. Corral and three of the cowboys died—Frank McLaury, Tom McLaury and Billy Clanton."

"I've read the story," Stanley said, glancing down at his notepad. "John Clum has nothing good to say about it. He wrote that 'the street battle between our peace officers and the rustlers was a grim exhibition that should have been omitted. The spectacle of men engaged in mortal combat is repulsive and distressing. It is inconceivable that any normal spectator derived either pleasure or benefit from viewing the fight. The lamentable clash between our peace officers and the rustlers on October twenty-sixth, 1881, occasioned more partisan bitterness than anything else that ever occurred in the community—and traces of the bitterness linger to this day. There was no justification for that gruesome act, and the good people of Tombstone surely find it reprehensible.' Those are very strong words, Sheriff Behan."

"I agree," Behan said. "The Earps are pugnacious, and so is Holliday. They were spoiling for a fight. John Clum did not tell readers both sides of the story. Wyatt is a boastful man, and he is given over to gambling and womanizing. The Earps wanted control of this town. Wyatt owns a gambling enterprise, and shares in some mining operations. He is not lily-white himself. I'm sure you know of his history in the Kansas cattle towns. Why, Wyatt had the gall to entice my wife, Josie, away from me, after I'd paid her way out here from back east. He's a man without principles. I'm sure you heard the story from Clum."

"Some of it," Stanley said. "I am hopeful that Wyatt will grant me an interview."

Behan frowned. "Both of his brothers are wounded. Now there's a new player in unfolding events who just came to town recently, a hired gun calling himself a medical doctor."

"Would that be Dr. Leo LeMat?"

"Do you know him?" Behan asked.

"I rode the trains with him out here from San Antonio. He is also an accomplished painter. I've seen some of his work, and I just learned today from John Clum that he accepted a job as interim city marshal."

"He what?" Behan exclaimed, leaning forward in his chair. "Who gave him the authority?"

"The Safety Committee. I understand there was

a meeting. Dr. LeMat accepted the job, according to Mr. Clum. I just spoke with him."

"Clum didn't even consult me!" Behan snapped. "What makes him think this picture-painting doctor can do anything about the trouble we're having?"

"Dr. LeMat has a most vicious reputation with a gun, Sheriff Behan. I learned about him while I was in San Antonio. He has killed a number of men."

"Clum takes his new position as mayor of this town too seriously. He's a Republican, like the Earps, and they stick together. Now he's hired a gunslinger to act as city marshal. What can anyone expect besides more trouble, more killings?"

"Tensions are still quite high in this town, even after the O.K. Corral incident," Stanley said.

"Higher than ever. This gunfighting doctor will only make things worse. I foresee more difficulties if LeMat goes after the cowboys. They won't take it lying down."

"You make it sound like your sympathies lie with the cowboys now."

Behan glanced at his office wall, the muscles working in his cheeks. "I hate that whole Earp family. Ever since they came here, we've had trouble. Wyatt is the worst of the lot. He's a greedy son of a bitch. There are some who believe Tombstone would be better off if the Earp brothers were dead."

Stanley picked up his notepad and a folded copy of the *Tombstone Epitaph* given to him by John Clum. The newspaper's headline read:

NEW INTERIM CITY MARSHAL, AN ACCOMPLISHED PISTOLMAN,
APPOINTED TO SETTLE INCREASING TENSIONS BETWEEN THE
EARPS AND OPPOSING FACTIONS.

"Thank you for your time, Sheriff Behan," Stanley said as he made for the office door.

Outside, he felt sure the *Epitaph*'s headline forecast a grim truth for residents of Tombstone. After meeting Dr. Leo LeMat and witnessing the incident in San Antonio with Bill Longley, it was almost certain that more blood would darken the streets of this city.

All Stanley had to do was seek an interview with Wyatt Earp and his brothers, if their present condition would allow it. A good place to start would be with Dr. LeMat. LeMat had been seen about town with Wyatt, so they knew each other by now.

Stanley rounded a corner, aiming for the Cosmopolitan Hotel. If what Sheriff Behan said about the cowboys' response to Leo's appointment as city marshal was true, he might not have much time to get an interview with Dr. LeMat before the gunplay started.

As he walked down the street, Stanley grinned

to himself. From what he'd seen in San Antonio, he'd put his money on LeMat.

Stanley knocked on Leo's door at the hotel. When Jacques answered it, a shotgun cradled in his arms, he could see Leo across the room working on a painting by the light from a northern window.

"Ah, Mr. Stanley," Jacques said. "It is good to see you again. Won't you come in?"

Stanley entered, letting his eyes fall to the shotgun in Jacques's arms. "Do you always answer the door armed?" he asked.

Jacques smiled. "These are dangerous times we live in, Henry, or haven't you been reading the newspapers?"

Stanley grinned. "That happens to be why I'm here, Jacques. The *New Yorker* magazine has commissioned me to write an article about the gunfight at the O.K. Corral and its aftermath."

Leo glanced up from his painting. "That will more than likely take a series of articles, Henry, rather than just one. It is a very complicated situation here in Tombstone."

"Would you care for a brandy?" Jacques asked.

"Yes, thank you," Stanley replied as he took a seat on a couch facing the corner where Leo was working.

"I agree the situation is complicated, Leo," he said, smiling his thanks as Jacques handed him a snifter filled with aromatic brandy. "But could you simplify it for me?"

"Certainly, Henry. It is a disagreement as old as civilization. The rights of townfolk are being pitted against the desires and wishes of those who live outside town, but want the services and benefits of the town to be available to them."

"You mean the cowboys?" Stanley asked.

Leo nodded. "The cowboys, and the ranchers who support them, like having a town that is growing as fast as Tombstone is, nearby. The problem is, the citizens of the town want it to become more . . . civilized as it grows, while the cowboys want it to remain wide open with few rules and even less law to impede their wild ways."

"And the Earps represent law and order?" Stanley asked, taking notes on a small notepad as Leo answered.

Leo grinned. "It's not that simple, Henry," Leo said. "The Earps do represent the law, but as in all things out West, it is law as they interpret it. And their interpretation is not always fair to all concerned, but is very subjective."

"You mean the friends of the Earps get special consideration under their enforcement of the law?"

Leo raised his eyebrows. "You sound surprised at that, Henry. In my experience, that is just the situation that exists in every city or town in which I've lived."

"That is a very cynical view, Leo."

Leo shrugged. "Cynical or no, it is the truth," Leo said. "Those people in any locality in power make the rules, and the lawmen enforce the rules in ways the powerful men want. It is not only the truth, it is the natural order of things."

Chapter 20

Ike Clanton was clearly drunk. It was early in the evening, a couple of hours before sundown. Leo was walking toward the Cosmopolitan with a newspaper under his arm and a bottle of good French wine in his fist. Jacques had gone to buy more cartridges and shotgun shells, insisting that they might need them now that Leo was acting city marshal, with Jacques as his official deputy. He expected trouble and plainly said so to Leo before he headed for the gun shop.

"Hey, you!" Clanton yelled, swaying to remain on his feet at a corner of Allen Street, staring at Leo with bleary eyes. He wore a gun belt high around his waist.

"Are you talking to me?" Leo asked, feeling his blood run cold, adrenaline rushing through his veins.

"Goddamn right I am, you phony bastard. We hear you took a job as city marshal. Heard it from a man who read it in the paper. You're gonna regret stickin' your nose where it don't belong! This ain't none of your affair."

Leo crossed the street. He came up to Clanton and stopped a few feet away. "It's refreshing to know that a filthy swine like you cleans out his ears once in a while. You indeed heard correctly. I'm the acting city marshal until the Earp brothers have recovered."

Clanton growled, his eyes narrowing. "A smart-ass remark like that can get you killed in this town. Nobody talks smart to a cowboy wearin' one of these red sashes."

Leo placed the bottle of wine and the newspaper near his feet. "Is that so? You can tell your cowboy friends they'd better get used to it. I intend to see that law and order are maintained in Tombstone. Any man who does otherwise will come to regret it. A red sash means nothing to me. I find it a rather silly decoration, in fact . . . something a woman would wear. But I assure you that a sash does not frighten me, nor will it turn me away from my duties."

"You're a smart-mouthed son of a bitch," Clanton said, his hand near the butt of his gun.

Leo took a deep breath. "That makes two insults you've given me. You called me a phony bastard, and now a son of a bitch. My dear mother, God rest her soul, would be deeply offended over the implications that I am a bastard and a son of a bitch. You leave me with no choice. I'll have to teach you a lesson in manners."

"You ain't gonna teach me shit, LeMat. We read all about you in the *Nugget*. You're a goddamn painter."

Leo took a quick stride forward and sent a powerful backhand across Ike Clanton's mouth. Clanton staggered backward a half step, eyelids fluttering as he fingered his bleeding lips.

Leo's teeth were clamped. "Are you just going to stand there and bleed, Clanton?" Leo demanded. "Or do you intend to go for that gun?"

"You can't do that to a cowboy," Clanton mumbled, wiping blood from his chin, regaining his balance.

"But I just did," Leo replied, controlling his temper as best he could. "I'm waiting for you to make a move for your pistol."

"That badge don't mean shit to us cowboys. We'll teach you a lesson or two about who runs this town. We'll be the ones holdin' school."

"Here's your chance," Leo hissed, taking another step closer to Clanton. "Reach for your gun. Or do you need someone else to do your fighting for you?"

"There's others. You'll see."

"Tell every one of them that I'm staying at the Cosmopolitan Hotel. I'm extending to every cowboy wearing a red sash a personal invitation to come and see me. And you can tell them one more thing . . . if another shot is fired at one of the Earps, I'll hunt every last one of you cowardly cowboy bastards down and kill you. You'll be one of the first on my list. I just gave you your chance to draw on me, and all you do is make more idle threats. You make an excellent bleeder, but a lousy hand with a six-gun. Now, take off that red sash, or I'm taking you to jail."

"You can't do that," Clanton stammered through his split lips.

"A new city ordinance was just passed today. The vote was held a few hours ago. Anyone caught wearing a red sash gets thirty days in jail. Take it off or you get thirty days behind bars."

Clanton glanced up Allen Street, his mouth oozing blood. "You ain't gonna get away with this. You're the same as dead."

"I'll take my chances. Take off the goddamn sash and drop it on the ground. It's the law in Tombstone now and I assure you I'll enforce it."

Clanton hesitated, then he reached behind him to unfasten the knot holding his sash around his waist. "You just started somethin' that's too big for you, LeMat," he said as the piece of red cloth fell around his ankles.

"Time will tell, Clanton. Now run down to the Red Dog and the China Tiger to tell all your friends about the new city ordinance. I'll have it posted in tomorrow's newspaper, and on signs all over town."

Clanton turned. "You're a dead man, LeMat," he said darkly before he stalked off.

Leo picked up his wine and paper and Clanton's red sash. "I've heard men say that before, Clanton. So far, all of them have been wrong. They sleep below ground in pine boxes, which is where I'll put you if you ever attempt to brace me again. I hope you have the good sense to remember what I said."

Ike stumbled into the Red Dog. He found Curly Bill, the tip of his ear crusted over with a bloody scab, sitting at a table in the back with Johnny Ringo, Hank Stilwell, and Ned Baxter.

"Bring your guns, boys," Ike snarled. "We're goin' over to the Cosmopolitan to kill that smart-mouthed doctor right now."

Ringo gave Ike a canted stare. "Why's that, Ike? Why do it now?"

"He said any cowboy who was caught wearin' a red sash from now on gets thirty days in city jail."

"What happened to yours, Ike?" Curly Bill asked.

"The sumbitch made me take it off. He was holdin' a gun on me or I'd have killed him," Ike lied. "He said it was a new city ordinance that red sashes wasn't gonna be allowed."

"Seems his recent appointment as actin' city marshal has gone to his head," Stilwell said.

"Let's gather up our shotguns an' kill him. Sheriff Behan won't say a word, since he's sidin' against them damn Earps. We can all claim it was self-defense."

"That wouldn't be smart," Ringo said. "We need to do it so no fingers of blame get pointed at us."

"What the hell are we gonna do, Ringo?" Ike demanded. "We gonna let that uppity dandy tell us we can't wear our sashes?"

"Ain't no man takin' my sash off me," Curly Bill said, tossing back a shot of whiskey. "I'll kill anyone who tries."

Ike Clanton snorted through his nose. "Yeah, Curly Bill. Just like you killed the man who cut half your ear off the other night."

Curly Bill glanced up at Clanton, noticing his lip was bleeding. "Hey, Ike. What'd you do to the man who busted your lip? I didn't hear no gunshots 'fore you came in."

"That was different," Ike protested. "I told you he had me covered with a gun."

Curly Bill nodded, a sneer on his lips. "I hear that sawed-off bastard who cut my ear off is Doc LeMat's deputy. Me and him have got a score to settle over the top of my ear. Right now, I'm busy drinkin'."

Ike motioned for Hank Stilwell and Ned Baxter to follow him outside and he turned on his heel and staggered drunkenly toward the batwings.

When they stood in front of the Red Dog, Ike lowered his voice. "Go fetch them shotguns. Bring one for me. Ringo and Curly Bill can stay here for all I care. I say we go kill this new city marshal right now. Johnny Behan won't do anything to us. He hates them Earps and all their friends as much as we do, on account of what Wyatt done takin' his wife away from him."

Hank nodded. "We'll meet you across the street from the hotel," he said. "Wait for us there. Stay out of sight. We'll bring the shotguns."

Stilwell and Baxter walked quickly toward the Dead Line, a poor residential section of Tombstone where they shared rented adobes.

Ike Clanton began weaving toward the Cosmopolitan with his mind made up to kill the new city marshal and get his red sash back.

"You're a dead son of a bitch, LeMat," he mumbled.

Jacques entered Leo's room burdened with packages of ten-gauge shotgun shells and cartridges. "Two men wearing red sashes are across the street talking to Ike Clanton. They all have shotguns."

Leo left his canvas to walk to a window. Dusk was settling over Tombstone. He saw Ike Clanton talking to two men he didn't recognize in the poor light. All three were cradling shotguns.

"My blood's at full boil, Jacques," he said.

"Let's go downstairs and take the sashes off those two, and whatever else they're willing to risk, including their lives."

"My sweet Ange is loaded," Jacques replied. "If we kill all three, they are worth fifty dollars apiece."

Leo opened his coat and took the hammer thong off his Baby LeMat. "I'll go out the front door. You come at them from the back, through the alley."

Jacques planted a kiss on the twin barrels of his Greener. "For good luck," he explained as they left the room.

Jacques headed for the back stairs.

"There he is!" Ike Clanton cried, bringing a shotgun to his shoulder just as Leo walked out of the hotel.

"Kill the sumbitch!" Hank Stilwell bellowed, taking his own careful aim.

Leo came out with his pistol. He fired once at Ned Baxter, the clap of a gunshot echoing up and down the street, his bullet sending Baxter spinning to the ground as people on both sides of the road began running for safety.

Hank triggered off a shot. The twelve-gauge shotgun's blast was muted by a much louder explosion behind him, lifting him off the ground, shotgun pellets shredding the back of his vest and shirt.

"I'm hit!" Hank shrieked as he went down with blood pouring from dozens of holes along his spine.

Ike Clanton whirled around with his shotgun to see who had fired the shot behind them. He saw Jacques standing a couple of dozen yards away, holding a smoking shotgun.

"Don't shoot him, Jacques!" Leo shouted from the front of the hotel, seeing the hesitation in Clanton's eyes.

Clanton threw down his shotgun, then he spun on his heel and took off in a lumbering run toward the saloon district.

Jacques ambled out of the alley. Women and children were running away from the scene in every direction down the boardwalks.

"Why did you tell me not to shoot him?" Jacques asked. "I could have killed him easily."

Leo strolled across the street, briefly examining the bodies of Stilwell and Baxter. Baxter was still alive, writhing on the gore-soaked ground around him. He would bleed to death in a few minutes.

"Clanton is our delivery boy, Jacques," Leo said as his temper cooled. "He'll carry word to Ringo and Brocius and the rest of them that we mean business about the ordinance."

"The ordinance?"

Leo chuckled mirthlessly. "Clanton wasn't wearing a red sash. These two are. I took Clanton's away from him earlier this afternoon. Let the word spread. A red sash in Tombstone means thirty days in jail for the man who's wearing it, or death for the man who refuses to take it off."

He holstered his pistol. "Find the undertaker," he told Jacques. "This one will be dead before the doctor's gurney can arrive."

He glanced over at Hank Stilwell, still writhing on the ground. "And you'd better call the doc for that one. It looks like he's going to live."

Jacques began to walk slowly up the street. "*Oui*, Leo, I will go to fetch the doctor, but I intend to take my time. With any luck, the bastard will bleed to death before I can locate the medical man."

Leo laughed as Hank Stilwell cried out, "Help. Get me some help. I been shot."

"Of course you've been shot, you stupid man," Leo said. "You appeared on the street carrying a weapon and wearing a red sash. If the doctor manages to save your worthless life, I'd advise you to tell all of your friends the consequences either of those two actions in this town from now on."

Chapter 21

Ike Clanton was out of breath by the time he reached Ringo and Curly Bill at the Red Dog.

"They shot Hank an' Ned!" he gasped.

"We heard the gunfire. Who shot them?" Ringo asked coldly.

"That sawbones who's the new city marshal, an' the little bastard wearin' the sailor's cap. I barely escaped with my life."

"You went after them in spite of my warning, didn't you?" Ringo remarked.

"I . . . reckon we did."

Curly Bill slammed his glass down on the table. "I'm gonna kill that short sumbitch! Look at my goddamn ear!"

"Not now," Ringo said quietly. "Wait until some of the others get to town. If we're gonna do this, we do it right."

"I say we kill Wyatt an' Morgan an' Virgil, too," Clanton said. "Time we got rid of all these lowly dogs. Sheriff Behan will back us up. Won't be no charges filed against none of us if we kill 'em all."

"That was my plan in the first place," Ringo said. "When the rest of the cowboys get here, we split up and take 'em down all at once . . . the Earps, that new marshal, and his partner. If we do it right, they'll all be dead in the same hour. We'll show folks who runs this town."

Clanton slumped into a chair. "We better do it quick is all I've got to say. That Doc LeMat thinks he's somebody special by makin' us take off our sashes."

Curly Bill gave Clanton a look. "You're the only one who ain't wearin' one. They'd better not try an' take mine or I'll drill 'em full of holes. I ain't like you, Ike. When a man challenges me, he'd better kill me before I kill him."

Ringo's pale eyes glazed over. "You didn't mind giving up part of your ear. . . ."

Curly Bill glanced away. "That was different. He snuck up behind me."

"We wait," Ringo said. "By tomorrow night, most of the boys should be here. Some of us will go after Wyatt and his brothers, while the others take down this marshal. If we do it right, they'll all be dead before midnight."

Jacques came to the door carefully with his pistol in his fist. "Who is it?" he asked, a hand on the doorknob.

"Sheriff Behan. I need to talk to Dr. LeMat."

"Let him in," Leo sighed, leaving his easel. "It doesn't appear I'll ever get the chance to paint Wyatt, or Holliday. Too many interruptions."

Jacques opened the door. Behan strode in wearing his finest business suit and a silk vest. He stopped a few feet inside Leo's hotel room with a hard look on his face. "You killed two men this evening, Dr. LeMat . . . or should I say Marshal LeMat."

Leo raised his eyebrows. "Two men? Only one was dead at the scene. The other was under the care of the local doctor when we left."

"Hank Stilwell died later, from blood loss, according to the doctor," Behan said.

"The man should have lived, and perhaps he would have if your doctor did not insist on trying to operate under the influence of the whiskey bottle," Leo said indifferently.

"Hank Stilwell was the brother of one of my deputies, Frank Stilwell," Behan said. "Frank is understandably upset."

Leo shrugged. "Then your deputy should have told his brother to obey the law and he would still be alive."

"Listen, LeMat, I am sheriff of Cochise County, with jurisdiction in such matters here," Behan said angrily. "I want an explanation. You aren't above the law."

Leo squared himself in front of the sheriff.

"Three men with shotguns came after me, Sheriff. There was a street full of witnesses. Ike Clanton threw down his shotgun and took off running, so I let him live. The others paid with their lives for assaulting a peace officer. If you wish to bring charges against me, I assure you I can fill a courtroom with people who will say that Jacques and I fired in self-defense."

"There are some who'll say otherwise."

"Then let them have their say in court!" Leo snapped, at the end of his patience with Behan. "And be forewarned. The next man who aims a gun at me will meet the same fate. I'm quite well-versed in the law, Behan. If you came here to threaten me, you've wasted your time."

Behan blinked. "What's this about some ordinance prohibiting the wearing of red sashes?"

"It was voted on and passed today by the mayor and the Safety Committee. Thirty days in jail for any man caught wearing a red sash inside the Tombstone city limits. Signs will be posted tomorrow, along with notices in both newspapers."

"It's a ridiculous law. It won't stand up."

"It has been approved by the city's highest officials," Leo said, trying to control his rising temper, "and I damn sure intend to enforce it."

"You'll be creating animosities," Behan replied. "You're a newcomer here. The cowboys won't like it. There'll be trouble."

"Then let the trouble begin," Leo said, jutting his jaw. "I assure you I'm fully prepared for it."

Behan turned on his heel to leave the room. "You're making a big mistake, Dr. LeMat, siding with the Earps. It won't make you popular."

"I didn't come here to win a popularity contest, Sheriff, or to get rich off stolen cattle, as some of the peace officers seem to be doing," Leo said, looking pointedly at Behan. "Now if you'll excuse me, I have work to do."

Behan was worried. He found Johnny Ringo and Curly Bill Brocius at the Alhambra having dinner. After looking around the dining room to see who might be watching, he came over to their table and took a chair.

"We have trouble in Tombstone, gentlemen," he said, speaking in a low voice.

Ringo nodded, as if he already knew. "You're talking about our new city marshal."

"Right. The mayor and the committee have given him a free rein. It's more than politics now, Democrats versus Republicans. LeMat has starting killing anyone who opposes him, and the committee has approved it, and he seems to know a whole lot about my business as well."

"You mean your added income from our cattle business, Sheriff?" Ringo asked, smiling tightly.

"He gunned down Hank Stilwell an' Ned Baxter," Curly Bill said. "Ike told us about it . . . he was there."

"I think it's time the cowboys took some action," Behan said. "Wyatt Earp and his brothers are behind this, and they have to be stopped before it's too late."

"We've already got a plan, Sheriff," Ringo said. "Why don't you leave everything to us."

"If you kill Wyatt and his brothers, along with this arrogant LeMat, order will be restored," Behan said. "I can't come out and do it publicly, however be assured you'll have my full support."

"We aim to do just that," Curly Bill said. "We're callin' in all the cowboys from the ranches. Virgil an' Morgan are wounded. Wyatt's still dangerous, but he's just one man. LeMat don't worry me none, and that sailor friend of his is a backshooter. Just ask Ike about it."

"It needs to be handled quickly," Behan urged. "Clum and his committee are behind them. I'm told LeMat and his deputy earn fifty dollars for every cowboy they have to kill. This has suddenly become a serious threat."

"We intend to take care of the problem," Ringo said with a forkful of steak in his mouth.

"Be careful of LeMat," Behan added, almost whispering. "I wired San Antonio, where he lives. The Bexar County sheriff said LeMat has a deadly reputation with a gun."

"I thought he came here to paint Wyatt's picture?" Ringo stated.

"He carries a business card saying his gun is for hire, and he apparently hired it out to the mayor and the committee until the Earps recover from their wounds."

"He's just one man," Ringo said. "He don't have eyes in the back of his head."

Behan gazed out a front window of the Alhambra for a time. "It has to be done soon. The wounded Earps are recovering. Doc Holliday is still around. If you add this Leo LeMat and his associate to the picture, this could wind up being a close fight over control of Tombstone."

"We'll take care of them," Ringo said. "As soon as the rest of the cowboys show up, we'll take care of our little problem with the Earps and LeMat."

Behan stood up, then he whispered to the two men. "I'll personally pay a hundred dollars in gold to the man who kills Wyatt. He's been a thorn in my side ever since he got here. I want him under snakes."

Ringo looked up from his steak at Behan, a smirk on his lips. "You think if Wyatt's dead, you're gonna have another chance at that wife of his, Josie?"

"That has nothing to do with it," Behan answered with heat. "The son of a bitch is trouble for all of us, not just me. He needs to be killed . . . soon!"

Behan strode out of the Alhambra with his hat tilted at a jaunty angle, certain in the knowledge that he had just signed Wyatt Earp's death warrant.

He whistled as he walked down the street toward his office. A major problem brewing in Tombstone had just been solved.

He crossed the road toward his office. If anyone could handle Wyatt and Doc Holliday, it would be Ringo. With enough men backing his play, Cochise County would soon be rid of a nuisance. Godfrey Gauss, the town undertaker, would be making a handsome profit in the days to come, and the steady income from looking the other way when cattle were stolen would continue to accrue in Behan's bank account.

Chapter 22

Henry Stanley was sitting at the bar in the Oriental Saloon, interviewing the bartender, Ned Boyle, about the events on the day of the gunfight at the O.K. Corral, when four men walked in through the batwings and stepped up to the bar.

"Whiskey, an' be quick about it," one of the men growled.

Stanley glanced at the men, noticing they were all wearing red sashes around their waists. He knew that meant trouble.

After Ned served the men their drinks, he walked back and leaned on the bar next to Stanley. They continued their talk of the day of the gunfight, Stanley making notes and trying to get the sequence of events correct.

After a short while, the men standing at the bar finished their drinks and threw some money on the bar.

One of them pulled his pistol out and opened the loading gate and spun the cylinder, checking his loads. He stared out the window of the Oriental Saloon and said, "All right, men, make sure you're loaded up six and six. We got us a marshal to take care of."

Stanley followed his gaze and saw Leo LeMat and Jacques LeDieux walking by on the boardwalk, deep in conversation.

After Leo and Jacques passed by out of sight, the four men loosened the guns in their holsters and walked slowly out of the batwings of the saloon, turning to follow Leo and Jacques.

"That don't look so good," Ned Boyle said, frowning.

"You got that right," Stanley said. "You got a gun here, Ned?" he asked.

Ned reached under the bar and brought out a short-barreled shotgun. "Just this old Greener," he said. "It's only good up to about ten yards."

"Give it here quick," Stanley said, hoping he wasn't too late.

Ned handed him the gun and he ran out the door, bursting through the batwings and turning the same way the cowboys had.

Fifty yards down the boardwalk, he saw the cowboys draw their guns, with Leo and Jacques twenty yards ahead of them with their backs turned.

Stanley eared back the double hammers on the shotgun and began to run down the street, stay-

ing off the boardwalk so the cowboys ahead
wouldn't hear him coming.

When the men raised their weapons, Stanley
held the shotgun at his waist and pulled both
triggers, yelling, "Leo, look out!" at the top of his
lungs just before the gun exploded.

Flame, smoke and molten buckshot roared
from the twin barrels, taking two of the cowboys
in the back and flinging them facedown on the
boardwalk, screaming in pain.

Leo and Jacques whirled around, Leo's Baby
LeMat appearing in his hand as if by magic while
the barrel of Jacques's Ange swiveled to point at
the cowboys.

Leo and Jacques fired simultaneously, knocking
the remaining two men to their knees, blood
streaming from multiple holes in their chests and
faces.

Suddenly, as gunsmoke billowed and swirled,
filling the air with the acrid smell of cordite,
blood, and excrement, it was over.

Later, back at the Oriental, Leo and Jacques sat at
a table with Stanley.

"You don't have to do this," Stanley protested.

"Henry," Leo said, "Any time a man saves my
life and Jacques's I insist on at least buying him
the best dinner to be had in the town."

"But it wasn't all that much," Stanley said. "It's
just that I cannot abide backshooters."

"Oh," Jacques said with a twinkle in his eye, "so our friendship had absolutely nothing to do with your heroic actions in firing on those desperadoes?"

Stanley grinned. "Well, to tell you the truth, if it had been anyone else they were after, I might well have contained my enthusiasm to watching the show, and to writing about it afterward."

Leo shook his head. "I do not believe that, my friend. You are much too honorable to allow anyone to be killed in such a manner, friend or no."

Stanley shrugged. "Perhaps you're right, Leo. However," he added, rubbing his right arm where the Greener had left a large bruise, "the next time I will confine myself to using a handgun instead of that cannon Ned gave me."

Chapter 23

It was an unseasonably chilly night, with frigid north winds blowing through the streets of Tombstone, when Leo and Jacques paid a visit to Virgil Earp's hotel room in the Cosmopolitan, where all of the Earps had been holed up since the threats by the cowboys. He removed the bandages and examined Virgil's leg.

The wound was already looking pink and healthier, with signs of gangrene vanishing. Virgil smiled up at Leo, his hands resting behind his neck and a cocky expression on his face. "Doc, I never would've believed it. Imagine, usin' worms to cure my leg."

"Medical science is always changing, Virgil," Leo said. "Who knows what we'll be doing next year? Hopefully, we'll be able to throw our saws away and be able to heal all bullet wounds as well as yours has."

"So, it's all right if I walk now?"

"Before long I dare say you'll be dancing," Leo

replied, putting his instruments away in his medical bag.

Virgil put his finger to his lips. "Hey, Doc, don't say that too loud or Allie'll be wantin' me to take her out on the town."

Leo shrugged. "It'd probably be good for both of you. Give you a chance to forget about all this cowboy nonsense."

As Virgil climbed out of bed to get dressed, Leo and Jacques said good-bye to Allie and walked over to the Oriental Saloon, where Wyatt was dealing faro.

Wyatt was sitting at a table with a brightly lacquered box in front of him, dealing cards to a variety of wranglers in town spending money they'd earned herding cattle on the trails leading past Tombstone, and miners flush with pockets full of silver.

"Howdy, Leo. Care to give the tiger a ride?" Wyatt asked.

Jacques was puzzled. "Ride the tiger?"

Wyatt grinned and pointed to a picture of a tiger painted on the front of the faro box. "That's what it's called when you play against the house, Jacques, because you have about as much chance of winning at faro as you would if you climbed up on the back of a tiger."

Leo took a seat before Wyatt and placed a roll of bills on the table. "Let's give her a whirl, Wyatt."

Wyatt shook his head. "I don't want to take

your money, Leo. Why don't you go over to the table where Doc's playing poker. At least there you'll have a chance of leaving with some of your money . . . as long as you don't bet against Doc."

Over the din of the drunken shouts and laughter of the revelers in the saloon, the distant booming of several shotgun blasts could be heard.

Leo looked at Wyatt. Wyatt grinned and shook his head. "Probably just a couple'a drunks celebratin' the coming of Christmas a bit early," he said, returning to deal to the players sitting in front of him.

A few minutes later, an ashen-faced Virgil stumbled into the Oriental Saloon and walked toward Wyatt's table, blood streaming from a fresh wound in his left arm.

Wyatt and Leo jumped to their feet, catching Virgil before he could fall to the floor. Leo quickly grabbed a nearby card player's bandanna and bound a tight tourniquet around Virgil's upper arm. He glanced at Wyatt. "Looks like a shotgun wound. We'd better get him to his room."

With Jacques's and Doc's assistance, the men struggled out the door and carried Virgil over to his hotel room, where they laid him on the bed. Allie cried softly in the background.

While Leo worked on Virgil's arm, Virgil motioned for Allie to come closer. He put his right hand on her neck and said, "Never mind, darlin', I've still got one arm to hug you with."

Later, after Virgil had been put to sleep with generous doses of laudanum, Leo addressed Morgan and Wyatt. "I'm afraid Virgil's fighting days are over. He'll never have the use of that arm again."

"Goddamn those cowboys," Wyatt said. He picked up his hat and said to Morgan, "Let's go see what we can find out."

Leo and Jacques accompanied the Earps to the site of the assassination attempt, easily located by the amount of blood in the street. Off to the side, Wyatt bent over and picked up a hat lying in shadows under the boardwalk. He turned it over and looked inside, then smiled grimly and handed it to Morgan.

Morgan read the name inscribed there: Ike Clanton. He glanced at Leo, a fierce look in his eyes. "That ornery coyote is as good as dead."

Leo drew his pistol and whirled around at the sound of approaching footsteps, only to see an elderly gentleman raise his hands, a frightened look on his face. "Hold on there, stranger. I got some news for the marshal."

Wyatt walked over to him. "What news?" he asked.

"I'm the night watchman at the gunsmith shop over yonder," the man said, pointing to a dark building. "After I heard the shots, I looked out the window and saw three men runnin' away."

"You get a good enough look at 'em to identify 'em?" Morgan asked, his voice tight.

"Sure. It was Ike Clanton, Frank Stilwell, and Pete Spence."

"You notice anything else?" Wyatt asked, making notes with a stubby pencil in a small notebook he carried in his coat pocket.

"Nope . . . other than the fact they was all carrying shotguns."

Leo and Jacques accompanied Wyatt and Morgan to Hatch's Pool Hall. What had happened to Virgil still weighed heavily on Leo's mind.

"Wyatt," he said as they walked through the darkness, "I'm afraid I'm partly to blame for what happened to Virgil tonight."

Wyatt glanced at Leo. "How's that?"

"One of the men Jacques and I killed last week was Hank Stilwell. Evidently he was brother to this Frank Stilwell, who attacked Virgil tonight."

Wyatt shook his head. "Don't let that worry you none, Leo. If Frank had been looking to get even for Hank's death, he'd have come after you, not Virgil. No, this is personal, between the cowboys and the Earps, and I promise you it won't end here."

When they came to Hatch's, they saw the pool table was unoccupied.

"Morg," Wyatt said, "you up for a little wager on a game of eight ball? Maybe it'll help take our mind off things 'til we can catch up to that back-shooter, Ike Clanton."

Morgan went to the wall and selected a cue stick from a rack. He glanced back over his shoulder at Wyatt. "Sure, brother. And since I've got this wound in my arm, you might even stand a chance of winning a few games for a change."

Leo ordered drinks all around as Wyatt removed his coat and got his own stick from the wall. Morgan racked the balls and stepped back from the table. "Hell, Wyatt, I'll even give you first break. Tomorrow, we're goin' after Ike and Stilwell and Spence . . . soon as it gets light."

Wyatt broke the balls, but nothing fell, so it was Morgan's turn. Wyatt sat back down with Leo and Jacques and took a drink of his brandy. "I'll probably be sitting here a spell. Morg's generally considered the best pool shooter in Tombstone. I still can't believe those sorry bastards ambushed Virge."

Leo said nothing, then he noticed Jacques glancing repeatedly at a large Regulator clock on the wall.

"Do you have an appointment to keep, my friend?" he asked.

Jacques's face flushed slightly and he cleared his throat. "I was thinking of attending the late show at the Bird Cage Theater to watch the lovely Fatima. She dances in a golden bird cage."

Leo wrinkled his nose and leaned closer to Jacques. "Is that Bay Rum toilet water I smell?"

Jacques nodded. "As a matter of fact, I have arranged to take the lead *artiste* in the show, Miss Fatima, to a late dinner at the Cosmopolitan after she is through entertaining."

"And just what sort of entertaining does she do?"

Jacques coughed and mumbled something.

Wyatt laughed. "He's right, Leo," Wyatt said, still chuckling. "Fatima is some pretty woman, and her costumes, or lack of them, have been a subject of considerable conversation among the menfolk of the town."

"I'm glad you agree with me about her attractiveness, Marshal," Jacques said somewhat stiffly. "Now if you gentlemen will excuse me, I must go to the Bird Cage Theater."

After Jacques left, Wyatt leaned across the table. "Your friend must have a great way with the ladies. Half the men in town have asked Fatima to spend an evening with them, and so far she hasn't taken any of their offers."

"Jacques can be most charming when the occasion demands it."

Wyatt took another drink of his brandy and watched Morgan sink another ball. "Hey, Morg. You gonna give me a chance to shoot?"

Down the street at the livery stable, Johnny Ringo took out a wad of greenbacks. Standing before

him in the shadows where casual passersby
wouldn't see them were Pete Spence, Frank Stilwell, and a Mexican woodcutter named Flo-
rentino Cruz, called Indian Charlie. Behind Ringo
stood Curly Bill Brocius, keeping watch to make
sure no one noticed them.

"All right, boys. Here's the money I promised
you for the job. And the rest of the cowboys
want you to know they'll be plenty grateful
for what you're doin' tonight."

Stilwell scratched his beard stubble. "I don't
know, Ringo. I don't much mind cuttin' a man or
two down, 'specially when they're as full of
themselves as the Earps are. But those brothers
stick together. I surely do hate to have the rest of
the clan, not to mention Turkey Creek Jack and
Texas Jack, on my trail for the rest of my life."

"Damn it, Frank, ain't nobody gonna know
who did this. The street's dark down by Hatch's,
an' we'll have some horses waitin' for you as
soon as it's done. By the time anybody realizes
what happened, you'll be at the south pass of the
Dragoons at Pete Spence's wood camp."

Stilwell shook his head, a worried expression
on his face, but he reached out and took the
money anyway.

The three men walked slowly down the boardwalk, keeping to shadows. Soon, they were
standing across the street from the rear entrance
to Hatch's Pool Hall. The back door had a large

window in it that offered a perfect view of the pool table the Earps were using.

"Looky there, boys," Spence said, pointing. "Morgan's shootin' pool an' Wyatt's sitting right next to him at a table."

"Who's that tall gent with the black coat sittin' next to Wyatt?" Stilwell asked.

"I don't have no idea," Spence answered, "but he ain't part of the deal, so you take a bead on Morgan an' I'll take a try at Wyatt."

Stilwell glanced at Cruz. "Indian Charley, you cross over there an' keep a watch on the street. You let us know if'n you see anybody comin' this way."

The Mexican nodded and stepped off the boardwalk to stand on the edge of the street, his hands in his pockets, whistling a soft tune.

Stilwell jacked a shell into his Winchester and Spence did the same. "We're only gonna get one chance at this, so don't miss," he whispered.

"Don't you worry 'bout me, Frank. I can shoot the eyes outta a squirrel at fifty paces. It's you we gotta worry about."

Both men glanced at Indian Charley, who nodded all was clear. They knelt behind a hitching rail and laid their rifles across it to steady their aim.

"Ready?" Stilwell asked.

"You bet," Spence answered.

Each man squeezed his trigger.

The rifles exploded seconds apart, shooting clouds of gunsmoke and flame into the night.

As Morgan leaned over to take his shot, the window of the rear door exploded, sending glass flying across the room. Morgan uttered a guttural grunt and straightened, his arm jerking behind his back as a hole appeared in his shirt over his backbone. A second shot followed, the bullet embedding itself in a post next to Wyatt's head missing him by inches when he tipped back his head to drain the brandy from his glass.

Morgan's body was flung forward and he landed on his face across the pool table, a crimson stain spreading across the white of his shirt as he moaned in pain and shock.

Wyatt and Leo flung themselves onto the floor, both hands filled with iron as they looked first toward the rear door, then back at Morgan.

"Oh, God . . . no!" Wyatt shouted, scrambling to his feet, ignoring the danger of another shot as he rushed to Morgan's side and grabbed him in his arms, cradling his head against his chest.

"Morg! Are you all right?" he cried.

Leo ducked low and ran to the rear door, peeking through the shattered glass in time to see three dim figures running up the street in the darkness. Two of them were carrying rifles in their hands, but he couldn't make out any of their faces.

He holstered his pistol and rushed over to the

pool table, taking quick note of Morgan's injuries. "It looks like the bullet shattered his spine, Wyatt. Let's get him up on the pool table."

The two men managed to turn Morgan over onto his back. His hand, bloody from his wound, reached up and grabbed Wyatt by the front of his shirt. "Wyatt," he croaked in a hoarse voice, "get my wife."

Wyatt looked over his shoulder to a group of men gathering from nearby pool tables. "Johnny, you and Jake run over to the Cosmopolitan and get my brother and our wives."

Leo looked up. "Be careful, gentlemen. The men who did this may be on their way to try to finish off what they started on Virgil, and to do the same thing to Warren."

He turned his attention back to Morgan, rolling him up on his side to get a better look at his wound. He stuck his finger in the bullet hole and ripped the shirt open, exposing a hole just over the middle of his spine.

Leo took part of the ruined shirt and stuffed it in the bullet hole to slow the bleeding, hoping to give Morgan enough time to see his wife before he died.

Wyatt, tears streaming down his cheeks, rubbed Morgan's cheek. "Hold on, partner," he said, his voice breaking. "Your wife's on the way."

Minutes later, Jim and Warren Earp entered the pool hall, along with a limping Virgil, whose face was still pale from the loss of blood from his arm wound. He was followed by the wives of th brothers.

The women, with the exception of Morgan' wife, stayed back, while all of the brothers gath ered around the table.

Virgil glanced at Leo, a questioning look in h eyes. Leo shook his head, indicating Morgan ha only minutes to live.

Morgan coughed, grimaced, and his hea slumped to the side, his eyes staring into eternit

Louisa threw herself on the table, wrapping h arms around Morgan's lifeless body and wailin as she rocked him back and forth.

Allie and Josie glanced at Wyatt, who wa watching with tears still streaming down his fa and his hands clenched into fists at his sides.

The women finally went over to Lou and gen tly eased her back from the table.

"It's all over now, honey," Josie said in a lo voice. "He's gone."

"Come on, Lou," Allie said, stepping to h side. "Let's go home now."

"Lou," Wyatt called as they started to leave.

She turned her reddened, flushed face to him

"I promise you, Lou, we'll get the bastards wh done this to Morg. The world ain't big enough f them to hide in."

Chapter 24

After the wounding of Virgil and the killing of Morgan, Wyatt and Warren Earp attended a coroner's jury investigating the events. Leo and Jacques, wearing their city marshal badges, stood at the rear of the room on either side of the door, feeling the remaining Earps needed protection from the vengeful cowboys.

Marietta, the wife of Pete Spence, was called to testify. She told the jury that her husband, along with Frank Stilwell and Indian Charlie, were the killers. She also stated that Johnny Ringo and Curly Bill paid them to do the job with money provided by Will McLaury, and that Johnny Behan knew of the plot and did nothing to prevent it from being carried out.

When she said this last, Wyatt jumped to his feet and pulled his pistol. He stared at the citizens serving on the coroner's jury. "There isn't but one way for justice to be served in a town where the law is an accomplice to murder, and this is it!" he cried, holding his six-gun up, waving it before the startled faces of the jury. "I aim to become judge, jury, and executioner to those who've attacked my family!"

Warren stood next to Wyatt, also staring at the men before him, until they turned and stalked out of the room without a backward glance.

Leo opened the doors of the courtroom for the Earps, and he and Jacques accompanied them to the Ritter and Ream funeral parlor, the same one where the bodies of Tom and Frank McLaury and Billy Clanton had been displayed.

Wyatt walked up to Jacob Ritter and asked, "Is my brother's body ready?"

"Yes, sir, Mr. Earp. We've got Morgan's casket all ready for the train ride."

"Good," Wyatt said shortly. "Put it in a buckboard and we'll take it to the station."

A crowd of men watched Wyatt and Warren load Morgan's body into the freight car on the now-repaired Tombstone rail line. When they were done, Leo walked up to him. "I hear you're going to ride as far as Tucson with the body, Wyatt."

Wyatt nodded. "Yeah. From there it's gonna be taken to Colton, California, for burial."

"Some of your friends," Leo said, indicating the crowd of men standing nearby, "fear there may be further attempts on your life when the train gets to Tucson. They've asked Jacques and me to come along and make sure nothing happens to you or Warren."

"Fine with me, Leo." He glanced at the pine box in the freight car. "Fact is, Warren and I could use the company of some good friends right now."

Wyatt and Warren climbed up the steps into a passenger car, followed by Leo and Jacques, Doc Holliday, Turkey Creek Jack Johnson, Texas Jack Vermillion, and Sherman McMasters. Wyatt had the conductor put them in a smoking car, with tables and chairs and its own bar. The men gathered around a large table, poured whiskey and brandy for everyone according to their tastes, and fired up stogies and hand-rolled cigarettes.

Leo quietly pulled a sketch pad from his valise and a long piece of charcoal. He positioned himself across from Wyatt and began to make a detailed drawing of his face, with small notations in the margins about skin, hair, and eye color.

Wyatt noticed his drawing and smiled crookedly. "You afraid I'm not gonna make it through the next few days to sit for your painting, Leo?"

Leo shrugged as he added in the outline of Wyatt's drooping handlebar mustache. "Who knows, Wyatt? It might just be that none of us will live to tell the tale of Tombstone and your infamous fight with the cowboys."

Turkey Creek Jack Johnson held up a water

glass full to the brim with whiskey. "I'll drink to that, boys!" he remarked.

Doc glanced at him as he raised his ever-present tin cup to his lips. "Hell, Turkey, you'll drink to damned near anything," he said in his soft, southern accent.

Leo finished with his outline of Wyatt and turned the page, shifting in his chair so he could do the same for Doc Holliday. The way Doc was putting brandy away, Leo was afraid if the cowboys didn't get him, the alcohol would. When Doc noticed Leo drawing his likeness, he didn't say anything, but Leo noticed that the ex-dentist turned his face slightly to the side, as if to hide the effects of his emaciation from tuberculosis.

The train pulled into the station at Tucson just after nine o'clock that night. Wyatt's friends exited first, forming a phalanx around him and Warren as they saw to the unloading of Morgan's body.

Suddenly, Wyatt whirled around and ripped Jacques's shotgun from his hands. "I just saw moonlight reflectin' off of two rifle barrels over behind that flat car," he whispered to Leo.

Leo leaned over and thought he could make out three or four shadowy figures crouched in the semi-darkness and mist of an evening fog. "Looks like there's a few men over there," he said.

"Sons of bitches!" Wyatt exclaimed and jumped over the tracks, heading toward the men.

Evidently they saw him coming, for they took off into shadows at a dead run.

Leo spoke softly. "You men stay here and guard Morgan's body. Jacques, you watch Warren's back. I'll go with Wyatt."

Leo pulled his pistol and followed Wyatt along the train tracks, both men moving fast in a crouched position to make themselves less of a target.

After about thirty yards, they caught up with one of the figures. "That's Frank Stilwell!" Wyatt whispered, recognizing his face illuminated in the glare of a locomotive's headlight. "One of the men who killed Morg."

Wyatt gripped Jacques's Greener shotgun in both hands, straightened up, and walked slowly toward Stilwell.

Stilwell shaded his eyes against the light from the train engine as he saw the tall man approach him out of the glowing mist. Suddenly his face froze in terror and he shouted, "It's the Earps!"

He took two steps backward, his hand disappearing inside his coat, his eyes glistening in the eerie light.

As he pulled his hand out of his coat, Wyatt let go with both barrels, and Leo fired several quick shots with his LeMat, then he flipped the lever and blasted Stilwell with the center shotgun barrel.

Stilwell's body jerked and turned and twisted in a frenzied dance of death under the impact of hundreds of molten balls and five well-placed .44 bullets.

When he toppled onto the rails, Wyatt whispered, "Serves you right, you son of a bitch!"

He glanced over at Leo. "Now, let's go find that bastard Ike Clanton and put an end to it."

They searched the train yard and its vicinity until almost three in the morning, but found no one.

"You know, Wyatt, by not sticking around and proving this shooting was self-defense, you've put yourself outside the law," Leo said as he held a match to Wyatt's cigar on the train back to Tombstone.

Wyatt took a couple of deep puffs. "The way I figure it, Leo, if I turn myself in to the authorities, I probably won't live long enough to stand trial." He chuckled. "And if by some miracle I do make it to trial, Behan and McLaury and their cronies will just make me a scapegoat."

The lawman shook his head. "No, by God, those bastards have forced me to ride this trail, an' I intend to ride it until every last one of the sons of bitches is in the ground."

* * *

The train pulled back into Tombstone just before noon, and the rail-weary men climbed down from the passenger car, rubbing sore bottoms and trying to keep their bleary eyes open long enough to find a bed upon which they could collapse.

A few hours later, Sammy Robinson, the town telegrapher, pounded on Wyatt's hotel room door at the Cosmopolitan.

Josie answered, holding her finger to her lips. "Please, be quiet. My husband's trying to sleep."

"Ma'am," Sammy said, tipping his hat. "I got this here telegram from Tucson tellin' Sheriff Behan to arrest Wyatt."

He handed her a piece of wrinkled paper, then, after looking over his shoulder at the empty hallway, said, "I can hold it for another hour or so, but after that I got to give it to him."

Josie reached in her purse and tried to hand Sammy some money, but he shook his head. "No, ma'am. I didn't do it for money. I did it 'cause Wyatt's always been good to me an' to this town. Tell him to shag his mount outta here 'fore Behan comes lookin'."

Josie woke up Wyatt, who, upon hearing the news of a warrant for his arrest, quickly got dressed and went to Warren's room just down the hall. As the two men readied to ride, Wyatt sent Josie to wake Leo and Jacques and let them know they were heading out of town before first light.

Chapter 25

Spring buds were beginning to show on wild flowers and trees as Leo and Jacques rode a trail in the Chiricahua Mountains with Wyatt and the rest of his friends.

They came to a crossroad high in a mountain pass and Wyatt reigned in. He twisted in his saddle, putting one leg over the saddle horn, and looked at Leo.

"Leo, you and Jacques have been good friends to me and mine. I want you to know I'd ride the river with you anytime."

Leo nodded. "That sounds like a good-bye speech, Wyatt."

"It is." The lawman pointed off to the right. "At the end of that trail lies Silver City, New Mexico. Now that most of the men involved in the killing and wounding of my brothers are dead, or run away, the boys and I plan to head on over there until this warrant foolishness calms down."

Leo looked down the trail to New Mexico with

mixed emotions. He knew his part in the saga of Wyatt Earp was at an end, but he had come to like and respect him. He briefly considered riding along, just to see what this extraordinary individual would do next to make life interesting. Finally, after a few moments, he decided they both had different trails to ride.

"Then I guess this is good-bye, Marshal," Leo said, sticking out his hand.

Wyatt wagged his head as he squeezed Leo's hand in a steely grip. "Maybe we'll meet again and I'll have the chance to sit for that picture like I promised you I would."

Leo glanced at the rolled-up pages of his sketch pad in his saddle bags. "I'll be able to complete the portrait from the sketches I made on the train."

Wyatt nodded. "Good. I wouldn't like to think I went back on my word."

While Jacques shook hands with Wyatt and the others, Leo spurred his horse over toward Doc Holliday. "Doc," he said, speaking low so the others wouldn't hear his words. "You cut back on those cigars and that brandy, and you'll live a lot longer."

Doc's lips curled in his trademark smirk. "Don't worry yourself none about that, Leo," he said in his lilting accent. "I intend to die with my boots on, not lying in some bed hacking my lungs up."

With that, Wyatt and his companions rode off toward New Mexico Territory.

As the sun approached the tops of the mountains to the west, Leo and Jacques came upon a small campfire built alongside the trail, a wispy plume of smoke whirling toward the sky from coals barely burning.

"Hello, the camp," Leo called as they dismounted their horses.

A crackle of underbrush and the snap of a twig signaled someone approaching from the forest on the side of the trail.

Leo turned just as Johnny Ringo stepped out of the cover, his pistol held at his waist pointing at them. He was barefoot and evidently had been in the bushes relieving himself when they arrived.

"Well, well, well," the outlaw growled, a nasty smile forming on his lips. "If it isn't the fancy-pants hired killer and his faithful companion."

Jacques's hand dropped toward the pistol in his belt, but Johnny cocked his gun and said, "I wouldn't do that."

Jacques scowled, but he let his hand relax, held away from his side.

"Now just what am I gonna do with you two?" Ringo asked, his grin widening. "Maybe I'll just gut-shoot you an' let the coyotes and wolves eat on your carcasses until you die."

Leo answered the threat with a smile, as if he

had no fear of that happening. He turned his head toward Jacques. "I guess Doc Holliday was right when he said Johnny Ringo was nothing but a two-bit saddle bum who never killed anyone who was facing him, and whose reputation was nothing but a pack of lies."

Ringo's face turned a dark red and his hand shook, as if the taunt was going to make him explode in rage. He managed to control his temper with obvious effort and stepped back.

"You," he said, looking at Jacques. "Pull out that six-killer with two fingers and throw it over here."

Jacques did as he was instructed.

"I don't want you making a stupid play," Ringo explained as he looked back at Leo. He stuck the pistol in his gun belt. "Now, Mr. fancy-pants . . . we're on even ground. Reach for that pistol and let's see who's faster."

Leo jerked his LeMat from his shoulder holster and fired from the hip without aiming.

Ringo was better than Leo had figured, managing to draw his gun and fire a split-second later than Leo.

Leo's bullet entered Ringo's forehead just above and between his eyebrows, snapping his head back and flinging him backward to land wedged in the fork of a blackjack oak tree, his arms dangling at his sides, his pistol in the dirt at his feet.

His eyelids fluttered and closed.

Leo glanced at the hole in the sleeve of his coat made by Ringo's bullet where it missed him by mere inches.

"*Mon Dieu, mon ami!*" Jacques exclaimed as he bent to retrieve his own pistol. "That man was almost as fast as you.'"

"There's a world of difference as wide as that between life and death in the word 'almost,' my friend."

Jacques laughed and pulled his dagger from his boot. He walked over to Ringo with the knife.

"What are you doing, Jacques?" Leo asked as he punched out his empty cartridge and replaced it with a fresh one.

"I intend to carry out a tradition of the local Indians, Leo."

He grabbed a handful of Ringo's hair and cut off a sizable portion just above the bullet hole in his forehead. Then he bent down, picked up Ringo's pistol, and attached it to the watch chain hanging from the dead man's vest.

Leo strolled over to Ringo's body, removed the city marshal badge from his own lapel, and pinned it on Ringo's vest. "I believe that's an appropriate place to leave our badges, don't you?"

Jacques nodded and pinned his badge on the other side of Ringo's vest. "Can we go home now?" he asked, wiping a trace of blood from his hands.

"We'll go back to the hotel and pack our gea
Make arrangements to have our coach coupled
the next train leaving Tombstone. Our business
finished here."

"*Bon, bon, bon,*" Jacques said, climbing aboa
his horse quickly. "I have never been so glad
bid *adieu* to a place. I thought there could be not
ing worse than Kansas, but I was wrong."

"I, on the other hand," said Leo, "would n
have missed this adventure for any amount
money."

"What is so good about a town of tents ar
shanties filled with men who dig in the dirt
day for a handful of shiny metal?"

"It is not the town or the townspeople that ha
made this trip worthwhile, my friend. It was t
chance to meet the Earps and Doc Holliday." I
glanced at Jacques as they spurred their hors
back down the trail toward Tombstone. "They a
the sort of men who are larger than life. I have
doubt they will live forever in the minds a
imaginations of future generations."

Authors' Note

Writing a novel can sometimes be a delicate balancing act. On the one hand the authors want to be entertaining, and on the other we want to be as historically accurate as possible.

While Leo LeMat and Jacques LeDieux are fictional characters, the setting of *Tombstone* and the remainder of the characters and their basic personalities and characteristics have been presented as accurately as possible.

Leo LeMat is fictional, but his "uncle," Dr. François LeMat, did exist. He invented a series of handguns called LeMats. These consisted of a circular cylinder holding nine bullets, surrounding a central barrel that fired grapeshot, and was of the approximate caliber of a twenty-gauge shotgun today. The LeMats were made for and carried exclusively by officers of the Confederate Army, and were generally considered to be the most lethal handgun ever produced at that time. Today, original LeMats are sold for upwards of six thousand dollars to serious gun collectors. The fascinating history of François LeMat and his revolvers can be found on several sites on the World Wide Web by typing in "LeMat" or "LeMat Revolvers" on any search engine.

In 1880, a bustling silver camp on Goose Flat was beginning to be called Tombstone due to the numerous gunfights and deaths among the miners who congregated there and for the size of its Boot Hill. Tombstone soon became a mecca for many different types of men: prospectors, real estate speculators, preachers, merchants, prostitutes, tin-horn gamblers, con men, and cattle rustlers.

James, Virgil, Wyatt, and Morgan Earp arrived from Prescott, Arizona, in December 1879. They were accompanied by their wives or companions, Bessie, Allie, Mattie, and Louisa.

In July 1870, Pima County Sheriff Charlie Shibell appointed Wyatt deputy for the Tombstone district. Almost immediately, he ran afoul of the notorious cowboys, headed at that time by Newman Haynes Clanton and his sons, Joseph Isaac (known as Ike), Billy, and Phineas, along with the McLaurys, Tom and Frank. The cowboy gang, which numbered over fifty, also included Frank Stilwell, William Brocius Graham (known as Curly Bill Brocius), and Johnny Ringo.

Ringo is often portrayed as a deadly, moody gunfighter who quoted Shakespeare. Other researchers claim he was really a two-bit saddle bum who never killed anyone. Some say he inflated his reputation to instill fear in his enemies. The truth probably lies somewhere in between.

Curly Bill was a tall, bushy-haired bully with coarse features, but he played the part of a friendly fellow who joked a lot. Though this made him popular with many factions in Tombstone, especially those who had other reasons for disliking the Earps, his sunny disposition hid the heart of a cold-blooded killer. It was he who took over the lead of the cowboys after "Old Man Clanton" was killed in an ambush by rival Mexican cattle rustlers in July 1881, just a few months before the OK Corral shoot-out.

Many of the other cowboys had come to Arizona in the 1870s from Texas to work as lawmen, some seeking employment from the famous Arizona lawman John Slaughter. Among these were Ringo, Curly Bill, Stilwell, and Billy Claiborne.

Wyatt got crossways with Johnny Behan when Behan was appointed as Wyatt's successor as deputy sheriff of Pima County. Perhaps Wyatt stole Behan's girl, Josephine Marcus, to get even . . . or perhaps he really loved her.

John Clum, in addition to being mayor, was editor of the *Tombstone Epitaph*, a paper that supported the Earps and was also involved with the Citizen's Safety Committee.

The opposing paper, the *Tombstone Nugget*, was owned by men who supported the cowboys and

Johnny Behan, and often portrayed the cowboys as "playful youngsters out having fun," even when that fun included riding roughshod through the town shooting holes in the canvas tents in which many of the townspeople lived and worked.

Josephine Marcus, known as Josie, wanted to be an actress. Johnny Behan spied her doing Gilbert and Sullivan in Prescott. Deeply in love, he followed her to San Francisco and persuaded her to return to Tombstone with him. After a while, Josie met Wyatt Earp, and soon Behan was history. Wyatt didn't let his arrangement with a woman named Mattie, who traveled from Dodge City to Tombstone with him, keep him from wooing and winning Josie.

Behan, furious with both Wyatt and Josie, never forgave either of them, and some say this is why he openly supported the lawless cowboys. In Josie's book, *I Married Wyatt Earp*, she shows how strange the relationship was between the law and the outlaws in Tombstone. She states that even in the midst of their troubles, while she was living with Behan and he was deputy sheriff, many of the cowboys, including Ringo and Curly Bill Brocius, came to the house to play poker with him. Stranger still, the night before the gunfight at the O.K. Corral, a poker game at the Oriental Saloon included Virgil Earp, Johnny Behan, Ike Clanton, and Tom McLaury. Perhaps it isn't politics that makes strange bedfellows, but poker.

There is plenty of evidence that Wyatt had in fact offered Ike Clanton a reward of six thousand dollars to bring Bill Leonard, Jim Crane, and Harry Head to a pre-arranged site where Wyatt could arrest them. When word of this agreement began to leak out, Ike became desperate. He was as good as dead if he couldn't convince the cowboys, now lead by Curly Bill, that Wyatt was lying in order to stir up trouble among the outlaws. The only way Ike could get back in the good graces of the cowboys was to force a showdown with the Earps.

During the days leading up to the O.K. Corral, Ike made several threats against the Earps, always making sure he was unarmed when he spoke out.

During the fight, after several shots had been fired, Ike ran up to Virgil and grabbed his arm, shouting that he was unarmed.

Virgil replied, "This fight has commenced. Go to fighting or get away." Ike turned and ran away, finally hiding behind a barrel of mescal in a dance hall several blocks away. So much for Ike Clanton's bravado.

Aftermath of the O.K. Corral:

On July 13, the body of Johnny Ringo was found at Turkey Creek, stuffed in the fork of an oak tree, a bullet in his head. His pistol hung from his watch chain with one bullet missing, and a piece of his hair was missing as if he'd been scalped. In typical Arizona fashion, the death was ruled a suicide. However, several people later claimed responsibility, including Wyatt Earp, Doc Holliday, Buckskin Frank Leslie, and even Johnny-Behind-the-Deuce O'Rourke. It seems the truth will never be known.

Ike Clanton moved north into the White Mountains, where he continued rustling cattle. In 1887, Ike was shot and killed by Rawhide Jake Brighton while running away, as usual, from a posse lead by famous lawman Commodore Perry Owens, sheriff of Apache County.

Phineas Clanton was captured and sentenced to ten years in the Yuma Territorial Prison.

Also in 1887, John Doc Holliday, while lying in bed in a hotel in Glenwood Springs, Colorado, asked for a shot of whiskey. After downing the whiskey, Doc, who'd always vowed he'd die with his boots on, glanced at his stocking feet sticking out from under the covers. He smiled, muttered, "This is funny," and died.

"Big Nose" Kate Elder finally split up with Doc and moved to Globe, where she opened a bordello. Kate, whose real name was Mary Catherine Haroney, died in the Arizona Pioneers' Home at Prescott in 1940.

Mattie Blalock, Wyatt's "companion" in Tombstone until replaced by Josephine Marcus, eventually moved to Pinal, where she was found in July 1888, dead of an overdose of laudanum and whiskey.

Johnny Behan, who, while working as a deputy sheriff, stole twenty-five thousand dollars a year in addition to his annual salary of twenty-five hundred dollars, was indicted by a grand jury for continuing to collect taxes after leaving office. Due to his political connections, he not only didn't do time for his theft, he was rewarded by being appointed superintendent of the Yuma Territorial Prison from 1887 to 1890 (interestingly enough, during the same year Phineas Clanton began his jail term there). He enlisted in the army during the Spanish-American War and later served in China during the Boxer Rebellion. He died in Tucson in 1927.

In July 1900, Warren Earp, the youngest of the brothers, was shot and killed in a barroom fight in Wilcox by Johnny Boyette. Even though Warren was unarmed, a jury ruled Johnny Boyette shot in self-defense.

Virgil and Wyatt continued to wander. Virgil and Allie stayed together while he worked as a marshal (in spite of his game left arm) in Colton, California, ran a saloon with Wyatt in Cripple Creek, Colorado, and Prescott, Arizona, where he again worked as a deputy sheriff. He was still

working as a lawman when he died of pneumo-
nia in Goldfield, Nevada, in 1905. Allie Earp died
in 1947.

Wyatt moved to Gunnison in 1882 and sent for
Josie, who'd gone back to San Francisco during
his days on the run immediately after Tombstone.
The next year he joined his old friend Luke Short
in the "Dodge City War." Some say it was his reputation that caused the other side to back down
without a fight.

Later Wyatt and Josie went to Eagle, Idaho, and
then to Cripple Creek to join Virgil in the saloon
business, along with stints involving race horses,
real estate and gambling.

In 1897, Wyatt again talked Josie into traveling
with him, this time to Alaska to search for gold in
the Klondike. After two years and $85,000 in prof-
its, the Earps moved to Tonopah, Nevada. It was
at this time that President Teddy Roosevelt's
press secretary, Stuart Lake, overheard Bat Masterson say the story of the true West would never
be known until Wyatt Earp decided to tell his
story.

After Masterson died in 1921, Lake sought out
Wyatt for his story. The result of his efforts would
be *Wyatt Earp: Frontier Marshal*, a classic blend of
truth and fiction that would turn Wyatt into a legend.

Only six years of Wyatt's life was spent as a

lawman, and he died peacefully in his sleep at 8:05 on the morning of January 13, 1929.

Josie stayed by his side for nearly fifty years and died in 1944 near her beloved San Francisco.

Ø **SIGNET**

Jason Manning

❑ **Mountain Passage**   0-451-19569-8/$5.99
Leaving Ireland for the shores of America, a young man loses his parents
en route—one to death, one to insanity—and falls victim to the sadistic
captain of the ship. Luckily, he is befriended by a legendary Scottish
adventurer, whom he accompanies to the wild American frontier. But
along the way, new troubles await....

❑ **Mountain Massacre**   0-451-19689-9/$5.99
Receiving word that his mother has passed away, mountain man Gordon
Hawkes reluctantly returns home to Missouri to pick up the package she
left for him. Upon arrival, he is attacked by a posse looking to collect the
bounty on his head. In order to escape, Hawkes decides to hide out among
the Mormons and guide them to their own promised land. But the trek
turns deadly when the religious order splits into two factions...with
Hawkes caught in the middle!

❑ **Mountain Courage**   0-451-19870-0/$5.99
Gordon Hawkes' hard-won peace and prosperity are about to be threatened by the bloody clouds of war. While Gordon is escorting the Crow
tribe's yearly annuity from the U.S. government, the Sioux ambush the
shipment. Captured, Gordon must decide whether to live as a slave, die as
a prisoner, or renounce his life and join the Sioux tribe. His only hope is
his son Cameron, who must fight his father's captors and bring Hawkes
back alive.

Prices slightly higher in Canada

Payable by Visa, MC or AMEX only ($10.00 min.), No cash, checks or COD. Shipping & handling:
US/Can. $2.75 for one book, $1.00 for each add'l book; Int'l $5.00 for one book, $1.00 for each
add'l. Call (800) 788-6262 or (201) 933-9292, fax (201) 896-8569 or mail your orders to:

Penguin Putnam Inc.   Bill my: ❑ Visa ❑ MasterCard ❑ Amex _____ (expires)
P.O. Box 12289, Dept. B
Newark, NJ 07101-5289   Card# _____
Please allow 4-6 weeks for delivery.   Signature _____
Foreign and Canadian delivery 6-8 weeks.

Bill to:
Name _____
Address _____ City _____
State/ZIP _____ Daytime Phone # _____
Ship to:
Name _____ Book Total $ _____
Address _____ Applicable Sales Tax $ _____
City _____ Postage & Handling $ _____
State/ZIP _____ Total Amount Due $ _____

This offer subject to change without notice.   Ad # N107B (6/00)